ANDREW V. KUDIN

I0591685

A HANDFUL OF SOIL

KUDIN & SONS
ACADEMIC PRESS

Chapter 1

Tony genuinely believed that life was nothing but a performance staged exclusively for him. It was obvious. The sun rose in the east purely for Tony's pleasure. Grass grew obediently beneath his feet. Women walked down Manhattan's avenues only to attract his gaze. Even beer bottles seemed arranged neatly on supermarket shelves solely to satisfy his whims. He was absolutely convinced that America was the epicenter of the universe and that he himself occupied the very heart of America. Any criticism from abroad aimed at his country felt suspiciously personal, like a subtle insult directed specifically at him.

That morning, Tony's alarm clock ripped through his dreams without mercy. At the exact same moment, his phone started buzzing angrily, as if it had plotted together with the clock to ruin his peace. Tony forced open one eye, cursed quietly, and fumbled around blindly, searching for the intrusive gadget. His fingers brushed against the remote, knocking it onto the wooden floor with a harsh clatter.

"Where the hell did I put the damned phone?" Tony muttered, finally pushing himself up and rubbing his tired eyes.

Beside him, the blanket stirred gently, revealing the warm skin of a woman's shoulder. Tony paused, watching with growing curiosity as the figure beneath the covers moved with lazy grace. She slowly lifted herself, allowing the thin white sheet to slide sensually down her back. Tony felt a sudden tightness in his chest as he admired her smooth curves, golden skin glowing softly in the morning sun, and thick black hair cascading carelessly across her slender neck.

The woman stood up without any hesitation, indifferent to Tony's attentive gaze, and moved effortlessly toward the bathroom. Each step she took was deliberate and hypnotic, her bare feet making almost no sound on the polished floor. As she reached the doorway, she paused for a moment, stretching her arms upward, arching her back in a way that ignited a surge of desire deep within him. Tony's breathing quickened. He'd always had a weakness for women like her—confident, graceful, mysterious—especially those with beautiful black hair.

But the relentless vibration of his phone drew him harshly back into reality. Irritation flared within him as he finally located it buried beneath yesterday's discarded shirt.

"What now?" he snapped into the receiver, barely restraining his frustration.

"Tony!" came Nancy's sharp, familiar voice, immediately erasing any trace of pleasant anticipation. Nancy was eight years older than Tony, his cousin, and mutual dislike had long become their family tradition. They spoke rarely, mostly under extreme circumstances, and each time was predictably unpleasant.

"Would it kill you to answer your damn phone?" she demanded angrily.

Tony yawned dramatically, holding the phone away from his ear. "Why are you yelling so early? How am I supposed to know it's you?"

"Early?" Nancy replied incredulously. "You mean you're still asleep?"

"What if I am?" Tony muttered irritably. He considered adding a few cutting remarks but restrained himself, knowing it was pointless. Arguing with Nancy was about as productive as shouting at passing clouds.

From the bathroom came the soft, seductive sound of water. Tony glanced toward the door, picturing Sofia—he vaguely remembered she had introduced herself with that name—under the warm streams. He briefly wondered whether she'd stay a while or quietly disappear as others before she had done, leaving behind only a faint, teasing scent and a few scattered memories.

"Honestly, Tony," Nancy said in her practiced tone of disdain, "I couldn't care less what you're doing—or who you're doing it with."

Tony clenched his jaw. He found it unbearable that Nancy's grating voice intruded upon this perfect morning moment, pulling him away from the enticing vision behind the bathroom door.

Nancy's voice lost its edge, now carrying weariness rather than anger. "You know, Tony, you were selfish as a kid, and clearly nothing's changed. Did you at least remember that today is Grandpa's funeral? Everyone's already at our house."

Tony froze momentarily, rubbing his forehead. Of course, now he remembered. Two days earlier, just before a critical business presentation, his mother had called him, her voice choked with tears. Tony had barely paid attention, promising hastily to call her back. Predictably, he never did.

His business presentation had turned into an enormous success, followed by champagne toasts, approving handshakes, and Sofia—or whatever her real name might have been. After that hurried call from his mother, Tony hadn't thought about his grandfather even once. He felt no grief now, only mild irritation at having to pretend sadness in front of relatives he barely recognized.

"Nancy," he finally replied, adopting a firm, confident tone, "just so you know, I haven't forgotten anything. Funeral at noon, church service afterward, and then that thing you do... What's it called again? A wake?"

"Whatever," Nancy snapped impatiently. "Just don't mess this up. Noon sharp—we're taking Grandpa's body from the funeral home to the cemetery. Try not to embarrass your mother again."

Nancy hung up abruptly without another word—as always.

Tony tossed the phone carelessly onto the crumpled pile of clothes, annoyed by Nancy's nagging and by the faint, unfamiliar sense of guilt creeping into his chest. His eyes lingered briefly on Sofia's pale dress, discarded carelessly next to his phone, before turning again toward the bathroom door, where steam now drifted lazily outward, inviting him closer.

He stood motionless for a few seconds, lost in the uncomfortable memory of the grandfather he'd barely known. Had it been two years, or maybe five, since he'd last seen him? God, how quickly time flew!

Shaking his head to banish the unwelcome thoughts, Tony decided that the only sensible thing left to do was to step into the shower. He'd join Sofia under the hot water, wash away any unpleasant residue of useless guilt, and reclaim this day as entirely his own.

Chapter 2

The funeral procession slowly passed through the heavy iron gates of the funeral home. Tony watched silently as the casket, completely covered by wreaths and bouquets, moved solemnly toward the waiting hearse. A long line of black cars followed behind, their headlights glowing softly in the gray autumn air.

As they drove toward the cemetery, Tony's thoughts circled anxiously around the strange power death held over life. It didn't matter how a person lived—rich or poor, famous or anonymous—death always had the final say. It transformed everything, painting life's familiar colors in darker, unknown shades. *Life is like a brightly lit stage*, Tony thought bitterly, *but death always waits in the shadows behind the curtain.*

When someone dies, Tony suddenly realizes that people always judge their life through the prism of death. First, they ask how a person died, and only afterward do they wonder how that person lived. It seemed absurd, almost unfair, yet deeply human. Death reshaped every story, turning ordinary people into mysteries and nobodies into heroes. Tony glanced again at the long line of cars trailing the hearse, genuinely puzzled by the sheer number of mourners.

He had never thought much of his grandfather—just a quiet old man living a dull existence in his modest suburban home. Yet here were dozens of people, respectfully dressed in black suits and formal dresses, their faces solemn, some openly grieving. It was unexpected and unsettling.

"Did I miss something important?" Tony asked himself, feeling suddenly uneasy. *"Or is this just tradition—people gathering out of habit?"*

Only when they arrived at the cemetery did Tony fully grasp what he had overlooked. They weren't burying his grandfather in some humble suburban graveyard but at Graceland Cemetery, in the heart of Chicago—a place reserved for the prominent and respected. Tony stood silently at the edge of the gathered mourners, feeling distinctly out of place.

His mother stood slightly ahead, shoulders trembling, her face pale and etched with grief. Tony knew he should stand beside her, comfort her somehow, but he couldn't bring himself to move any closer. The shame was too strong, the guilt too real. He hadn't even called her back when she'd needed him most. A sudden pang of remorse shot through him, sharp and heavy, as he watched her silent suffering.

The air grew colder, carrying with it the unmistakable scent of autumn—damp leaves, cold earth, and the metallic tang of rain. Tony shivered and tightened his coat, growing increasingly restless. Death hung over them like a heavy, oppressive fog, smothering them with its harsh truth. Low, heavy clouds pressed down upon the city as if Chicago itself mourned silently alongside them.

"How much longer can this possibly take?" Tony wondered impatiently, glancing around as the priest continued solemnly reading from the Bible.

Then, slowly, the coffin began its descent into the earth. People stepped forward one by one, tossing handfuls of soil into the grave. Each clump landed on the coffin with a dull, final sound, echoing sharply in Tony's ears like muffled gunshots. The dark earth symbolized everything Tony had tried to avoid—finality, loss, regret. He stood frozen, unable to join them, unwilling to pretend grief for a man who was essentially a stranger despite their shared blood. The wind grew stronger, slicing through his coat, carrying the scent of wet earth and decay.

Without consciously deciding, Tony quietly stepped away from the crowd, unnoticed by anyone. He slipped past the mourners, past the line of cars, past rows of gravestones bearing carved names. By the time the others had returned to their cars, ready to drive to the church for the wake, Tony was already walking quickly in the opposite direction. He didn't say goodbye; he didn't even glance back at his mother or relatives.

He just kept walking, unwilling—to look back.

Chapter 3

The next morning, Tony's mother called and asked him to come over. Tony immediately felt awkward, remembering how abruptly he'd left the funeral without even saying goodbye. A wave of guilt washed over him; he hadn't considered his mother's feelings at all when he quietly slipped away from the cemetery. At that moment, he'd wanted only one thing—to escape the ceremony that depressed him and forget it as quickly as possible.

Despite his discomfort, Tony knew he couldn't refuse. After a brief hesitation, he got into his car and drove south.

Tony's mother lived several miles south of Chicago in a quiet neighborhood where life felt simpler and property taxes weren't as high. Her house was the third one on the left after the intersection.

It was the only home in the neighborhood surrounded by flowers. Tony paused in front of the porch, inhaling deeply. The fragrance was rich and familiar, bringing back memories he'd nearly forgotten. Everything here was unchanged: the wooden steps with their faded paint, the slightly crooked railing he'd once swung from as a child. He felt as if he'd stepped into a different time, into a world he'd long left behind.

His eyes wandered to the small garden overflowing with asters, blooming brightly despite the early September chill. Gardening had been his mother's quiet refuge, a solitary passion she had lovingly cultivated for decades. As a boy, he often watched her from the porch, noticing the joy in her eyes as she bent over the flowerbeds. The asters seemed magical to him then—vivid splashes of yellow, pink, purple, and blue, colors so intense they appeared to glow.

One particular afternoon came sharply back to him. He must have been five or six, angry over something trivial, when he'd torn off dozens of blossoms, scattering petals and leaves across the living room floor. His mother had discovered the damage almost immediately, and Tony could never forget the silent anguish on her face. She'd covered her eyes briefly as if shielding herself from physical pain, whispering only, "What have you done?"

She hadn't shouted, hadn't punished him—yet that quiet, wounded look haunted him for years. Tony wondered now if she felt the same quiet disappointment over him missing the wake.

His mother sat on the porch, wrapped in a knitted shawl. She looked small and fragile, seated in a worn black lawn chair he recognized from his childhood. When she saw him, a gentle smile lit her tired face, though her eyes remained deeply sad.

"I'm so happy you came," she said softly. "I always worry you'll forget me altogether."

Tony shifted uneasily, guilt rising in his chest. He hadn't realized just how long it had been since his last visit.

"I wish you had joined us at the church," she continued gently, looking away. Her voice carried no anger, only a quiet sorrow that stung Tony more sharply than any harsh words could. "Afterward, everyone came back here. We read your grandfather's will."

Tony tried to hide his boredom behind a yawn, but his mother noticed and frowned slightly.

"Tony, I know this doesn't interest you," she said, a note of gentle reproach in her voice, "but your grandfather mentioned you specifically."

"If you mean that ancient Buick or the decrepit shack you call a ranch—I don't want them," Tony snapped, immediately regretting his harshness.

She shook her head, patiently ignoring his tone. "The house didn't go to you. But the rest of his estate did. Everyone was shocked when the lawyer read that part of the will."

Tony raised an eyebrow skeptically. "Estate? Grandpa had something besides debts?"

His mother gave him a quiet, almost apologetic look. "He left you over two million dollars, Tony. Two million eighty thousand, to be exact, plus accumulated interest."

Tony felt his heart skip a beat, disbelief flooding through him. He stood abruptly, nearly stumbling backward.

"Two million dollars?" he repeated, incredulous. "Where did he get that kind of money? He wasn't exactly a gangster. Grandpa was just an ordinary old man who barely stepped out of his—" He stopped abruptly, suddenly aware of the harshness of his words. "...His house," he finished awkwardly.

His mother sighed quietly, her gaze distant. "He was a complicated man, Tony. Someday, you might understand him better—when it's your turn to face him again. For now, just know the money is yours. What you do with it isn't my business, but I think it would be fair if you shared some with Nancy."

Tony scoffed softly. "Why should I? Nancy never did anything for me."

His mother clasped her hands tightly in her lap, the lines in her face deepening. "Tony, Nancy is the only relative who still speaks to you, even if you rarely answer her. She has a husband and two kids to raise, their college tuition looming ahead. They love you, even if you hardly know them."

A pang of guilt shot through Tony again, sharper than before. He hadn't seen Nancy's family in years. Memories of missed birthdays, unanswered invitations, and ignored phone calls suddenly crowded his mind. He sat back down heavily, dropping onto the porch next to his mother and resting his head lightly on her shoulder, something he hadn't done since childhood.

"Two million dollars..." he murmured, more to himself than to her. "It's absurd."

She placed her hand gently over his. "Your grandfather was deeply private. Even I barely understood him."

The silence grew heavy between them. Tony desperately wanted to ask her more—about his grandfather, about her, about everything he had ignored for so long—but the questions stayed painfully trapped in his throat.

Sitting there beside his mother, Tony felt a deep emptiness inside him, an uncomfortable awareness that something crucial had passed him by unnoticed. His entire life had been a race without purpose. Expensive clothes, fast cars, luxurious watches—things he collected mindlessly, without ever pausing to question why he needed them. Now, facing his mother's quiet grief and his grandfather's strange generosity, his carefully built confidence wavered, leaving him feeling suddenly lost and exposed.

Chapter 4

Tony and his mother stepped into the house together from the front porch. Inside, just like outside, nothing had changed. Tony slowly glanced around the familiar living room, feeling that any careless movement might shatter the fragile illusion of his childhood.

His mother gently leaned toward him and kissed him softly on the cheek.

"I've missed you," she whispered.

Tony tensed involuntarily but quickly forced a smile. "I missed you too," he replied.

The words felt empty, rehearsed, and awkward. He remembered clearly that last year, he hadn't even bothered to call her on her birthday.

A heaviness settled in Tony's chest, and he suddenly found it difficult to breathe. Feeling suffocated, he stood up abruptly and walked toward the window, avoiding his mother's calm, searching eyes. He imagined silent reproach in her gaze, though she said nothing to accuse him. His throat tightened with frustration, guilt, and confusion. His eyes drifted to his grandfather's photograph and then to the paintings depicting scenes of Ukraine—a distant and foreign country he'd never paid attention to before. Unable to contain his emotions, Tony turned abruptly, his voice sharper than intended.

"Mom, why didn't you ever talk about our family's past? About Ukraine, for example? Why didn't you ever tell me that's where we came from? Does it even matter?"

His mother took a deep breath, her shoulders slumping under the invisible weight of unspoken memories.

"It just happened that way," she finally answered. "Maybe because the past was too painful. I've never been to Ukraine; we were all born here in America. Our lives have always been here. When you work all the time—from morning till night—you don't have room for memories."

She paused, looking at Tony with tired eyes. "You're a college graduate; you have a steady job in aviation. When I was young, I couldn't even dream about college. Life was different then. Even though your grandfather made sure we had enough food, we never really forgot what poverty felt like."

Tony frowned, struggling with something he couldn't clearly identify. "What about Grandma?" he asked quietly.

"She died when I was three," his mother answered softly. "Your grandfather always blamed himself because he couldn't provide me with a proper education. He promised himself that his grandson would attend the best schools. He was proud when you got in, but he was disappointed you never truly appreciated it."

"I didn't know," Tony whispered helplessly, his voice trembling slightly.

"It's not your fault," she replied softly. "Like so many other immigrant families, we spent so much time working for our children's future that we forgot to spend time with them." She looked away briefly, tears quietly filling her eyes. "That was our mistake, Tony."

Tony shook his head stubbornly. "But I'm not an immigrant. I'm not Ukrainian. I'm completely American. You were born here too—we're Americans, Mom."

His mother smiled sadly. "I used to think exactly the same way. But America was built by immigrants. Some came long ago, others just yesterday. Whether you accept it or not, Ukrainian blood runs through your veins."

A tense silence filled the room. The candle beside his grandfather's photograph hissed softly, casting flickering shadows on the wall. Tony stared at the old photograph and finally broke the silence.

"Mom, why did Grandpa leave Ukraine?"

She took another deep breath, carefully choosing her words. "Life was unbearable then. Grandpa was the oldest child. His father first went to Argentina to earn money. When he finally sent money home, there wasn't enough for everyone's tickets. Your great-grandmother had to make a terrible choice. One of the children had to be left behind. Grandpa stayed in Ukraine because he was the oldest. He was about eleven at the time. After two years, the family finally saved enough money to send for him, and Grandpa joined them in Argentina."

"How did he survive those two years alone?" Tony asked, amazed.

"Grandpa never shared details. He only mentioned once that monks from the Kiev-Pechersk Monastery took care of him. After that, he became deeply religious. He often said, 'You can't escape your fate.' When life was difficult, he always repeated, 'Never mourn what you lose. Life is about losing and gaining, and what truly belongs to you can never be lost.'"

She paused, wiping away a tear. Tony felt an unfamiliar ache in his chest.

"Later, the family moved from Argentina to the United States. I was born in New York, and then we moved here. We avoided talking about Ukraine—there was too much pain, too many tears. But now your grandfather made it clear in his will that he wanted you to go there. Honestly, I'm glad he did."

Tony raised his eyebrows. "Why?"

"It means he cared about you. That he believed in you."

Tony stood silently, troubled, staring again at his grandfather's photograph.

"Mom, who else might know about the two years Grandpa spent alone?"

"No one," she replied sadly. "Everyone who might have known is already gone. He left something behind in Ukraine, something he searched for his entire life, something that haunted him until his last breath. Maybe you'll find the answer there, at the monastery."

A chill ran through Tony. "Mom, what are you talking about?"

She flinched slightly and looked away. "I'm afraid, Tony. It sounds foolish, perhaps—but I have a bad feeling. It's almost as if you won't be going to Ukraine. Instead, it will be your grandfather returning, using your body."

Tony stared at her, confused. Pushing away his unease, he forced himself to speak rationally.

"What do two million dollars have to do with Ukraine? Is the money buried there or something? What exactly am I supposed to find?"

His mother laughed softly. "No, the money isn't buried anywhere. It's in Grandpa's bank account. The lawyer will explain everything. As for what you'll find in Ukraine, I don't know. Maybe you'll understand when you get there."

She quietly left the room and returned, holding a cardboard box.

"This is everything I have left from Grandpa—photos, letters, bits and pieces of his life. Maybe this will help you." She hesitated. "Did you ever wonder why we named you Tony?"

"No," Tony admitted. "I assumed it was because we lived among Italians."

"No," she smiled gently. "Your grandfather insisted on it. Tony comes from Antonius, a Latin name meaning 'one who enters into battle.' Grandpa used to say that Kiev was the heart of Ukraine, and that the Kiev-Pechersk Monastery, founded by Saint Anthony, was the heart of Kiev. He wanted you to carry that strength." She paused, hopeful. "Will you stay for dinner?"

Tony shook his head softly. "Not tonight, Mom. Maybe next time."

They stepped outside together—a frail, aging woman and a strong young man holding a box filled with memories.

"Tony," she whispered, almost inaudibly, touching his sleeve. "Think carefully before you decide. I'm scared. No one knows what's waiting for you there."

Tony smiled reassuringly. "Don't worry. I'll talk to the lawyer first; maybe I won't have to go anywhere. Besides, work won't wait."

When his car disappeared around the corner, she stood alone on the empty street, finally letting the tears flow freely.

"You think you're the one making the decision about going," she whispered into the darkness. "But you're wrong. It's already been decided for you. You can't hide from what's waiting."

Chapter 5

On his way home from his mother's house, Tony stopped by a bookstore and bought a world map. He wasn't entirely sure why since he could easily find everything he needed online. Still, Tony wanted a physical map—something he could hold in his hands, unfold, and touch—not just an image on a cellphone screen. It was a strange, inexplicable impulse.

Back at his apartment, Tony carefully unfolded the map and spread it across the coffee table next to the cardboard box his mother had given him.

He paused, uncertain of what to do next. The shrill ringing of his phone jolted him from his thoughts.

"Hello? Sophia? Hi, sweetie. Listen, I'm a bit busy today," Tony said, immediately regretting turning her down. "I'll call you tomorrow, okay?"

After hanging up, Tony felt a pang of regret. Sophia's long, beautiful black hair and smooth, warm skin always made him feel better. Perhaps her company could have calmed the strange unease that was now settling over him.

His eyes drifted back to the cardboard box. On impulse, he tore off the tape, opened the lid, and emptied the contents onto the table.

Sitting down, Tony absently sorted through the old, yellowed photographs of strangers who'd probably been gone for decades, faded postcards depicting pre-revolutionary Kiev, a worn bus schedule, and a broken button.

Just as his mother had said, these were fragments of a past life—useless to others, yet priceless to the one who'd kept them, filled with stories Tony would never fully know.

His intuition told him that somewhere in this clutter lay the key to understanding what his grandfather had wanted to tell him.

There were no letters or clear records left behind; his death from a heart attack had taken everyone by surprise.

Beneath the photos lay an old map Tony hadn't noticed at first—a small, neatly folded sheet of sun-bleached paper. He opened it eagerly, hoping it held some clue, but was disappointed. It was merely an ordinary tourist map of the Kiev-Pechersk Monastery from the early twentieth century. He examined it carefully, turning it over several times, but found nothing unusual—no marks, notes, or hints.

As Tony sorted through the contents of the box, a thunderstorm rolled in. Distant peals of thunder rumbled through the house. For a moment, he thought he heard footsteps, but it was just the pounding of heavy rain on the roof. A shadow moved swiftly across the room, and suddenly, a strong gust of wind hurled a tree branch against the kitchen window. Glass shattered loudly, followed by the faint clink of shards hitting the floor.

Tony jumped to his feet and hurried into the kitchen. The small window was completely broken, shards of glass glittering across the floor. Carefully picking them up, he tossed them into the trash and returned to the living room. As he wiped his hands on a towel, Tony noticed a small cut on his finger. Droplets of blood had fallen directly onto the world map—right onto Ukraine.

Chapter 6

Grandpa's lawyer turned out to be an exceptionally smug gentleman with high-waisted pants and a triple chin. Tony had never realized lawyers could be so irritating.

The lawyer cheerfully paced around his desk, occasionally handing Tony documents to sign. Every now and then, he would pause to mention how wonderful it was to have such a charming, handsome young man among his clients and how close he'd been with Tony's late grandfather. Then he'd promptly remind Tony how fortunate he was to have such a remarkable lawyer as himself.

If it weren't for the money, Tony would've shown the lawyer and his stack of endless papers straight to the door. Instead, he patiently signed every sheet and nodded at all the appropriate moments.

The paperwork seemed endless. When the lawyer finally handed him the last document, Tony signed it with visible relief. The lawyer gave him a self-satisfied smile and neatly placed the papers into a folder. Tony felt as if he had just awakened from a long, exhausting dream.

"Congratulations!" The lawyer shook Tony's hand eagerly. "It was such a pleasure to meet you. I never doubted your grandfather would have a grandson worthy of handling his affairs. You remind me so much of him, God rest his soul."

"Yeah, nice meeting you too," Tony replied skeptically. "Can I have my money now?"

The lawyer's smile widened. "No doubt about it—the money is yours! Well... after you put a handful of earth on your grandfather's grave."

"For that kind of money, I'd put a whole bucket of earth on his grave," Tony remarked sarcastically. Yet the thought of anything standing between him and three million dollars was unsettling, even if it was just a handful of earth. Suddenly, he remembered that at the funeral, unlike the rest of his family, he hadn't thrown any earth onto his grandfather's coffin.

The lawyer stopped twirling his pen and gave Tony a strange look. "My job as your grandfather's lawyer is simply to inform you of what's written in the will. You must bring back a handful of earth from your ancestral homeland. Only then can you claim your inheritance."

"So, let me get this straight," Tony said. "I have to go to Ukraine, bring back a handful of dirt, put it on my grandfather's grave, and only then can I have the money?"

"That's exactly right."

Tony shifted uneasily, suddenly feeling embarrassed. "Okay, but how will you even know if I actually brought the earth from Ukraine—or from anywhere else, for that matter?"

"I don't need to know exactly where it came from. Honestly, I don't particularly care whether you really bring back any earth at all. All I require is a copy of your passport with a Ukrainian border stamp. How long you stay there doesn't matter. Just the stamp—nothing more."

Tony paused thoughtfully. "Is there any way I could claim the inheritance without traveling halfway across the world?"

The lawyer firmly shook his head. "I'm afraid not. You should also know that if you fail to bring back the earth within one year, the entire sum automatically goes to charity. I have the documents here if you'd like to look them over."

"Thanks, but no thanks," Tony sighed, realizing the conversation had ended.

The lawyer rose from his seat, politely escorting Tony to the door.

"Think of it this way," he added cheerfully, patting Tony on the shoulder. "Take a short vacation. Soak up the atmosphere and relax a little. Personally, I'd love to travel somewhere myself—it's been far too long since I've had a proper break."

Tony nodded automatically in response, already drifting into his own thoughts.

Chapter 7

Tony was well-known at the travel agency; he was one of their regular customers. A young woman smiled at Tony from behind the counter, a wide grin making her already round face even wider.

"Going on safari to Africa again this year? Or maybe somewhere closer? We have great deals on trips to Jamaica," she said with a heavy accent.

Her petite build and almond-shaped eyes intrigued Tony. Perhaps the owner had brought her from Vietnam or Thailand. Foreigners always seemed elusive to Tony; he could never tell whether they had green cards or were in the country illegally.

Because of her accent, it took Tony a moment to realize what she was saying. "Actually, I want to go to Kiev this time." Seeing the confusion in her eyes, he repeated slowly, "Kiev. I need a round-trip ticket to Kiev."

"Oh, great!" She finally seemed to understand and nodded enthusiastically. "You're sure to love it there. Which airline would you prefer?"

Tony shrugged. "Which airlines do you have?"

"Just a minute," she said, studying her computer screen. "There's a Japanese airline available. Would you like that?"

Tony stared at her, puzzled. "Japanese? Japanese airlines fly to Kiev?"

"Of course—excellent service and great prices. Actually," she added with a nervous smile, "you'll have a connecting flight in Los Angeles. I hope that's not a problem. It's a great deal. Should I book it for you?"

Tony hesitated, still confused. He wanted to fly east, not west— but then again, the Earth was round... Glancing at the large world map hanging on the wall, he felt something didn't quite add up. Leaning forward over the counter, he looked at the woman's screen.

"Wait a minute. I asked for a ticket to Kiev," Tony repeated slowly, syllable by syllable. "Kiev—not Tokyo. I don't need Japan. I need Kiev, Ukraine!"

The woman's face showed utter confusion. Her gaze darted helplessly between Tony and the monitor several times.

"So you're... not going to Tokyo?" she finally asked quietly.

Tony felt his patience running thin. "Maybe some other time. Right now, I have to get to Kiev."

Without another word, the young woman abruptly disappeared into the back room. Tony couldn't understand how anyone could vanish so quickly. "Definitely from Vietnam," he thought. "They have jungles there—everyone moves fast."

She reappeared just as suddenly, her boss following close behind her. He was a tall, heavyset American man in his fifties. Standing side by side, the two of them seemed oddly amusing to Tony. The young woman reminded him of a nervous Pekingese dog, while her boss resembled a calm, reliable Newfoundland.

"Hey, Tony," the owner greeted him, trying to sound friendly. "How's life?"

"Sometimes good, sometimes bad," Tony replied dryly. "Life is life."

"Right," said the owner, adjusting his glasses. "Life is life. I'm sorry, but we don't specialize in trips to the former Soviet republics. I can refer you to one of our partners who can help."

He pulled out a notepad and scribbled down a phone number. Tony noticed the man was left-handed. Recently, he'd begun noticing small details that had never interested him before.

"You'll need a Ukrainian visa to enter Ukraine," the owner continued, handing Tony the slip of paper.

The young woman quickly dialed a number and passed the phone to her boss. Tony suddenly realized her value to the agency—she handled things swiftly and, more importantly, quietly.

After a short conversation, the boss handed the phone back to her. "Yes, you'll definitely need a visa. Contact the Ukrainian consulate here in Chicago. They'll probably direct you to another travel agency that can organize everything. Our partner's contact details might be helpful. If you call them, mention my name—they'll give you a good discount."

Tony slipped the paper into his back pocket and shook the owner's hand.

"If you change your mind, it's the perfect season for South Africa," the boss said cheerfully. "An elephant safari is much more exciting than a trip to Ukraine."

"Thanks," Tony replied sarcastically, "but I've got my own safari."

Chapter 8

The Ukrainian Consulate in Chicago was not hard to find. In the early 2000s, it occupied the basement of an elegant but noticeably aged three-story building at the intersection of East Huron and North State Streets. Behind a low iron fence, painted a dull, peeling black, stood a slightly rusted flagpole from which a yellow-and-blue Ukrainian flag fluttered lazily in the autumn breeze.

Tony descended the short staircase into the cramped, dimly lit waiting room of the consulate. The low ceiling seemed to press down on visitors, and the air inside was stale, smelling of old paper and dust. A few worn chairs were arranged haphazardly, and several visitors stood huddled around a small service window, waiting with visible impatience.

Behind the glass barrier, a tired-looking young man was engaged in an increasingly tense conversation with a distraught woman. Her passport had expired, and the consul was adamantly insisting that she return to Ukraine to obtain a new one. The woman waved her arms emotionally, repeating that she had a stable job and a devoted husband in America. Leaving the country, she argued, would destroy both her career and her marriage to a man she proudly called "an American patriot."

Her husband stood silently beside her, a tall, unimpressive man wearing an old baseball cap. Nervously chewing gum, he nodded uncertainly as she gestured in his direction.

The other visitors watched the scene in weary silence. One older man glanced irritably at his watch. A younger woman impatiently shuffled through her papers, counting them now and then as if hoping their number would magically decrease.

Behind the consul, shelves sagged under piles of documents, folders tumbling chaotically onto the narrow desk. The consul rubbed his forehead, took a deep breath, then waved Tony forward with a tired motion of his hand.

"I need a Ukrainian visa," Tony began, trying to speak cheerfully despite the oppressive atmosphere.

The consul yawned, his eyes dim with fatigue. "Business or private?"

"Private," Tony replied, forcing himself to smile politely.

The consul slid a form through a narrow opening under the glass. "Fill it out, please. Indicate whom you intend to visit and where you will be staying, and enclose a letter of invitation on the back."

"I don't have an invitation," Tony admitted uncertainly.

The consul raised his eyebrows slightly and smiled weakly, humorlessly. "Then at least write down whom you're visiting and why."

Tony hesitated, feeling increasingly uncomfortable. "Actually, I don't know anyone in Ukraine."

For a brief moment, Tony saw a genuine look of surprise on the consul's haggard face.

"Then what is the reason for your trip?"

Tony shrugged, suddenly feeling awkward under the stares of everyone present. "Just sightseeing, I guess. I've never been there."

Behind him, Tony heard a quiet chuckle. He turned slightly, noticing a middle-aged woman with brightly painted lips who quickly averted her gaze, covering her mouth with a handkerchief.

The consul slowly shook his head and sighed again—this time even louder. "Sir, you don't need a private visa. You need a tourist visa. I assume this is your first visit to Ukraine?"

"Yes," Tony confirmed, his voice sounding quieter now.

"In that case," the consul explained tiredly, "you should contact a travel agency first. Before we can issue a tourist visa, we need proof of accommodation, your itinerary, and proof that someone will receive you upon arrival. After you've settled these matters, please come back. Next!"

Tony felt panic rising in his chest. His pulse quickened as he imagined being disinherited over some bureaucratic nonsense. "Wait," he interrupted desperately, leaning closer to the glass. "Could you at least give me the address of a travel agency that deals with Eastern Europe?"

The consul stared at Tony for a moment, clearly annoyed. He glanced at the clock on the wall and waved vaguely toward the doorway.

"There's a shelf near the entrance, to your left. You'll find the addresses there. Next!"

Tony stepped back, feeling an unpleasant heat rise in his face. Turning sharply, he headed toward the indicated shelf. A neat stack of colorful brochures and business cards lay covered in a thin layer of dust. Tony grabbed a handful and impatiently shoved them into his coat pocket, his hands trembling slightly with frustration.

Stepping outside into the cool Chicago air, Tony stopped and took a deep breath. The pressure of the consulate, with its thick, stifling bureaucracy, gradually began to ease. Still, he felt a tightness in his chest, an anxiety he had rarely experienced before.

Chapter 9

Tony found the travel agency quickly enough, though he'd never had any reason to stop on Devon Street before. It was a street of contrasts: half was filled with bustling Russian grocery stores and cafés frequented by immigrants from the former Soviet republics, and the other half was occupied by brightly colored Indian and Pakistani shops filled with the aroma of curry and incense. If you wanted 220-volt electronics or multi-system appliances in Chicago, Devon was the place to go.

But the agency Tony entered wasn't at all like the vibrant shops around it. Its poverty was conspicuous: a dimly lit office cluttered with outdated furniture and tourist posters that had long faded in the sunlight. Behind a messy desk sat a woman of indeterminate age with long, bright-red fingernails. The smell of cheap perfume mingled unpleasantly with stale sweat in the air.

Behind her desk, a map of the world was taped to the wall, labeled in a language Tony couldn't identify. Next to it, cassette tapes and CDs lay scattered haphazardly among various pamphlets. They clearly weren't American; Tony guessed they were Ukrainian or perhaps Russian—though he couldn't distinguish between the two cultures. In his mind, it was all one mysterious world somewhere far away.

Seeing Tony standing in the doorway, the woman reluctantly put aside the foreign magazine she'd been leafing through and slowly rose to greet him. Tony immediately sensed her irritation, as though he'd distracted her from something more important than her job.

Without warning, the woman reached out and firmly grasped his hand as if afraid he might run away. The gesture made Tony extremely uncomfortable. He fixated on her unnaturally bright fingernails, trying to free his hand as inconspicuously as possible. It was difficult to concentrate on her words; her very presence was oddly distracting.

"Can I buy a tour to Ukraine?" Tony asked.

"Yes, of course! I'm originally from Ukraine myself."

"Really?" Tony finally managed to free his hand and stepped back cautiously. "You're Ukrainian?"

"What are you talking about? I'm American!"

Tony raised an eyebrow. "Yeah? And how long have you lived in America?"

"Six years!" the woman replied proudly.

"And would you like to go back?" Tony asked, half curiously, half provocatively.

She laughed dismissively. "Are you kidding? Why would I want to go back?"

To prevent her from grabbing his arm again, Tony picked up some brochures from the desk and pretended to flip through them. He barely glanced at the glossy pictures, mostly keeping an eye on her movements.

"How long do you plan to stay in Ukraine?" she asked in a businesslike tone, clearly eager to make a sale.

Tony paused uncertainly. "I don't know yet. Maybe two days, maybe five."

She immediately clasped her hands together and shook her head emphatically as if the idea of such a short visit was absurd. "No, no! Why so short? You can't fly halfway around the world just to stay for a couple of days! We work with one of the best agencies in Ukraine. They'll handle everything perfectly—transfers from Boryspil airport, hotel reservations, city tours..."

"Wait a minute," Tony interrupted sharply. "What's Boryspil?"

"It's the international airport in Kiev," she explained patiently. "You'll change planes in Frankfurt am Main and then arrive directly at Boryspil. Believe me, Ukraine is worth at least a week of your time. Kiev alone has amazing museums and incredibly beautiful churches, like the Kiev-Pechersk Monastery—"

Tony shuddered, suddenly wary. Out of the corner of his eye, he saw—or thought he saw—a shadow flicker across the walls of the shabby office.

"What did you just say?" Tony asked suspiciously, looking around uneasily.

The woman gave him a perplexed look. "I said 'monastery.' Why? Is something wrong?"

"No," Tony muttered quietly, still distracted. "Just thinking out loud."

Shaking off the strange feeling, Tony tried to refocus as the woman opened another brightly colored pamphlet and jabbed at it decisively with a red fingernail. "Look at this. You really should consider at least a week—maybe even two. Yes, it'll cost a little more, but you'll get so much more out of the trip. If you like architecture, we could even include an excursion to Lviv. It's a beautiful city with old European charm. What do you think?"

Tony hesitated again, torn between suspicion and practicality. "I'll think about it," he said slowly. "But what about my visa?"

The woman laughed lightly as though he'd said something amusing. "What's there to think about? That's exactly why we're here. Our agency exists so clients don't have to worry about anything. Just relax—we'll handle the visa, flights, hotel, and everything. So, do we have a deal?"

After a brief internal struggle, Tony nodded. "Fine, let's do it."

Without wasting a moment, the woman quickly booked his tickets, accepted his check, and gently but firmly ushered him to the door. When she opened it, her expression brightened, and she smiled warmly for the first time since he'd walked in. "I'm sure you'll become a regular customer."

Tony nodded politely and walked out, hearing the door close behind him.

A muffled voice came from the agency's back room. "Well, how did it go?"

"How do you think?" the woman replied cheerfully, nearly laughing. "He only wanted one week, but I easily sold him two!"

Chapter 10

Tony sat on the couch with his laptop resting on his knees, slowly flipping through articles about Ukraine. He'd started with travel sites full of vivid pictures and enthusiastic recommendations, but soon drifted into reading about the country's history. The more he read, the darker his expression became. Ukraine's past seemed like an endless series of upheavals: revolutions, famines, wars, economic disasters, the collapse of the Soviet Union, and years of violent conflict. It was as though this land had been cursed, its people experiencing everything except happiness.

Lost in thought, Tony didn't immediately notice Sofia emerging barefoot from the bedroom, wearing only one of his old shirts, her hair still slightly damp from the shower. She moved quietly through the living room, a steaming cup of coffee in her hands, and curled up on the couch next to him.

"What are you reading about so seriously?" she asked gently, blowing softly on her coffee to cool it.

"Nothing important," Tony replied absently, adjusting his glasses to reread a paragraph.

Sofia leaned closer, her warmth comforting against his shoulder. "Want some help?"

Tony took a deep breath, removed his glasses, and rubbed his tired eyes. "Thanks, but no. I'm just trying to figure something out."

"Figure out what?" Sofia asked softly, sipping her coffee. Her voice was calm and soothing.

Outside, through the half-open window, the familiar sounds of a Chicago evening drifted into the apartment: distant sirens, the soft hum of passing cars, snippets of conversation in Spanish floating up from the street below. The curtains gently stirred in the cool evening breeze.

Tony hesitated, then turned the laptop slightly toward her. "Look here. Ukraine became independent and abandoned socialism in 1991, right? After that, it should have gotten stronger, richer—at least as much as Poland or the Baltics. But instead, in the first decade of independence, its population shrank by more than four million people. And it wasn't due to wars, famine, or disease. People simply... disappeared. I don't understand. Why is the country shrinking, dying?"

Sofia shrugged slightly. "There's nothing strange about it. Many countries faced trouble after independence. Look at Africa— after they kicked out the colonizers, people immediately started fighting each other, setting back development for decades."

Tony shook his head gently in disagreement, placing his glasses back on his nose. "But Ukraine isn't Africa. It's right in the heart of Europe. Still, no one considers it European."

She smiled faintly, taking another slow sip. "European or not, people have problems everywhere. Maybe your Ukrainians haven't figured out who they are yet. Sometimes people just don't know what to do with freedom. It's sad, but not unique. Maybe they don't even need freedom. From what I read online, they've always been serving someone."

With these words, Sofia gracefully rose from the couch and walked leisurely toward the kitchen, the shirt brushing lightly against her thighs. Tony's gaze lingered on her briefly before returning to the screen. Left alone, he tried to organize his thoughts about Ukraine and the upcoming trip.

On one hand, Tony felt genuine curiosity—the quiet excitement of discovering a new world, of finding roots he'd never known he had. On the other hand, a troubling sense of unease gnawed at him, hinting that this trip would offer more than just sightseeing and pictures.

He took another deep breath. If it weren't for the money, he definitely wouldn't be going. Time had always felt precious to him. This thought had settled deep inside him since childhood. Money could buy many things, but never time.

Reading about Ukraine, Tony sensed that life was measured differently there. In America, life had always seemed valuable, priceless even. Yet in Ukraine, life appeared cheap. Tragedies like Chernobyl seemed disturbingly commonplace. The fact that kindergartens were fed substandard food bought by corrupt officials at triple the price, or that pharmacies openly resold expired medications, shocked no one. What seemed horrifying to an American was apparently normal in Ukraine.

It occurred to Tony that Ukrainians perhaps viewed life through a darker prism and lived by entirely different moral principles.

On the other hand, if Wikipedia was to be believed, Ukraine had gifted the world countless brilliant minds—musicians, poets, scientists. Yet instead of protecting them, Ukraine had imprisoned, executed, or exiled many. And somehow, inexplicably, new generations continued to rise as if from the ashes.

Tony's thoughts returned again to his grandfather. Who was this man, really? How had he thought and lived? Most importantly, why had the old man insisted Tony visit this distant land?

His grandfather had named him Tony after Saint Anthony of Pechersk—the very Anthony whose monks had saved his grandfather's life nearly a century ago. Tony's mind wandered back to the faded, old map of the Kiev-Pechersk Monastery he'd discovered among his grandfather's belongings.

"Sofia," he called out loudly toward the kitchen, "do you like monasteries?"

"What do you mean?" Sofia's voice floated back through the doorway. "Are you asking if I could become a nun?"

"Sort of."

"Not my style," she laughed softly. "Not yours either."

Tony carefully closed the laptop, leaned back on the couch, and rubbed his temples. "Not mine either," he echoed quietly.

Chapter 11

Sofia had insisted on accompanying Tony to the airport, but he kindly refused, claiming he had too many things to finish before leaving. Now, standing alone in his quiet apartment and mechanically packing his suitcase, Tony felt an uncomfortable pang of guilt. Maybe he should've agreed to let her come along. The apartment seemed colder without her warmth, without the familiar aroma of her perfume floating gently through the rooms.

He paused for a moment, staring blankly into the open suitcase. Strange, he thought, how life worked. A chance encounter with a woman whose name he barely remembered at first had turned into something meaningful—something Tony was reluctant to label, even to himself. Sofia had quietly, effortlessly become a part of his life, a woman whose presence was always felt, even when she wasn't there.

What troubled Tony most was Sofia's ability to remain perfectly calm on the surface, regardless of her true feelings. It was almost impossible to guess whether she was upset, angry, or hurt. She had wished him a good trip with a quiet smile and a soft kiss on the cheek, showing no sign of disappointment at his decision to go alone. If only she'd expressed sadness, irritation—anything—it would've made things easier for him. Instead, she wore a mask of serenity, one that slipped only in those quiet moments they shared in the darkness of the bedroom.

Tony sighed heavily and ran a hand through his hair, catching his reflection in the hallway mirror. Usually confident, even arrogant, he now saw something unfamiliar in his eyes—uncertainty.

He checked once again that the documents from the travel agency—his flight confirmations, itinerary, visa, and credit cards—were securely tucked into the left pocket of his jacket. Everything was ready.

His gaze fell on the suitcase. At the very bottom lay a cardboard box containing his grandfather's yellowed photographs, postcards, and the old, faded map of the Kiev-Pechersk Monastery. Tony knew that Kiev had changed greatly over the decades, but perhaps among those aging images he'd find something familiar, something to cling to when he arrived in that strange city.

He zipped up the suitcase and listened to the quiet hum of traffic from the street below, mixed with the muffled sounds of laughter drifting in from a neighbor's open window. Life here went on as always, simple and predictable. Yet, Tony felt as if he were already someplace far away, someplace unfamiliar.

***

Tony had always had an inexplicable fondness for airports. He loved their restless energy. Every time he traveled by plane, he felt an intoxicating excitement- as if something better, brighter, and more meaningful was waiting for him on the other side of the flight.

But today, uncertainty crept into that familiar feeling.

Tony moved slowly toward the check-in counter, dragging his carry-on bag behind him. It was uncomfortably hot in the terminal, and he could feel a thin layer of sweat protruding under his shirt. He stopped briefly outside the café, inhaling the soothing aroma of freshly brewed coffee, and thought about buying a bottle of water. But the line was too long, and he quickly dismissed the idea. Besides, security would take it away at the checkpoint anyway.

He glanced at his watch.

The airport was humming with typical morning chaos. A calm female voice broadcasts announcements of flight delays and gate changes over the loudspeaker. Small children scurried between rows of seats, their mothers following behind with a tired expression. Through the large panoramic windows, airplanes landed and took off, shimmering gracefully in the morning sunlight.

Tony paused to watch the rhythmic ballet of the planes and felt a sudden, uncharacteristic tightness in his chest.

Shaking off the feeling, he pulled his boarding pass and passport from his pocket and held them out to the guard.

"Excuse me, sir," the airport employee standing next to the guard said and stepped forward. "Your bag is too large for carry-on luggage."

Tony raised an eyebrow skeptically, irritation rising in him. "I always fly with this bag. It fits perfectly in the overhead compartment."

"Sorry, sir," the airport employee repeated firmly, not looking particularly apologetic. "Those are the rules. You'll be able to pick her up at your destination."

The clerk's indifferent tone was getting on Tony's nerves. He wanted to object, but when he saw the stony expression on the young man's face, he realized it was pointless - after all, he was just doing his job. Irritated, Tony bent down to quickly shift his belongings. When he opened the bag, several magazines fell awkwardly to the polished floor. Tony bit his lip to suppress a swear word, and as he bent down to pick them up, his jacket slipped and fell to the dirty floor.

He impatiently grabbed his jacket and, without thinking, stuffed it mechanically into the bag in place of the magazines.

With exaggerated politeness, the guard returned Tony's passport and boarding pass. "You may pass."

The airport attendant placed Tony's bag on the conveyor belt, and soon it was out of sight.

Squaring his shoulders, Tony threw a dismissive glance at the guard and strode briskly toward the gate.

***

The plane shuddered and swayed as it sped through the darkness above the Atlantic Ocean. From time to time, Tony felt a sharp jolt, as if invisible hands were shaking the massive machine. Above him, the "Fasten Seatbelt" sign blinked insistently, flooding the cabin with an unsettling amber glow.

Tony tightened his seatbelt and peered out the window, searching in vain for something familiar in the endless void. Shifting uncomfortably, he felt a wave of anxiety rising in his chest. Noticing a flight attendant passing by, Tony remarked, "It seems to be shaking more than usual tonight."

The attendant paused and leaned slightly toward him. "This is perfectly normal. We're just passing through an area of turbulence. Right now, we're flying over the North Atlantic Ridge, which lies beneath the surface of the Atlantic Ocean. The turbulence should pass soon. There's nothing to worry about."

He nodded, more to reassure himself than out of genuine agreement, and watched as she continued down the aisle, balancing effortlessly with the plane's movements. Tony tried once more to settle into his seat, but sleep—which normally came so easily during flights—stubbornly refused to come.

Instead, he lay awake, tense, his mind fixating on every creak and groan from the airplane's metal frame.

Again he leaned toward the window. His breath fogged the cold glass as he stared out into the darkness. Outside, there was nothing—only blackness stretching endlessly, deeper and darker than he'd ever imagined. Not a single star, not even a distant glimmer of moonlight. For a brief, unsettling moment, Tony felt they weren't flying through air, but drifting helplessly through some unfathomable, impenetrable void.

Pulling away from the window, he rubbed his tired eyes. The uneasiness inside him deepened. Tony glanced around the dimly lit cabin. Some passengers slept peacefully, oblivious to the turbulence, while others shifted nervously in their seats, just as restless as he was. With a quiet sigh, Tony closed his eyes.

Chapter 12

Borispol, Ukraine's main air gateway, turned out to be a small provincial airport, modest and nondescript. Tony didn't even see any of the large airplanes he was used to in Chicago.

Initially, Tony felt cheerful as he waited for his luggage. Passengers from his flight from Frankfurt had already collected their bags and departed. Yet, for some reason, his suitcase was nowhere to be found. Even travelers who arrived after he had retrieved their luggage left Tony standing alone near the baggage carousel.

Glancing at his watch, Tony felt his stomach tighten in disbelief. Frustrated, he decided to find an airport employee, suspecting he might have misunderstood something or was simply waiting in the wrong place.

When Tony finally spoke with the airport clerk, the young man wasn't at all surprised by his situation. Politely but indifferently, he guided Tony to a service counter and quickly returned to his duties. Tony got the impression that nobody in Ukraine was in as much of a hurry as back in Chicago. People here wore serious expressions, burdened by worries, rarely offering a friendly smile.

During his Internet research about Ukraine, Tony had developed the idea that Ukrainians were hard workers but perhaps didn't know how to enjoy life. They seem perpetually engaged in overcoming difficulties, locked in a constant battle for survival. He wondered if happiness had ever really been part of their vocabulary.

Several other unfortunate travelers were gathered at the lost luggage counter. The clerk behind the desk acted less like an airport employee and more like a psychologist, calmly reassuring irritated passengers that their belongings would eventually turn up. His favorite advice was to go get some sleep and save their nerves—after all, nerves weren't something you could replace easily.

When Tony finally reached the desk and handed the clerk his ticket, the man slowly typed something into his outdated computer, studied the screen, then said calmly, "One minute, please."

Tony breathed a sigh of relief, assuming this meant his luggage had been found nearby. But his hope vanished quickly.

"It seems your suitcase is still in Frankfurt," the clerk sliding a slip of paper across the counter toward Tony.

Tony stared at the paper in disbelief. "What's this?"

"Our phone number," the clerk explained patiently. "Call tomorrow or maybe the day after. We'll let you know when your luggage arrives."

Tony felt his throat tighten. "Tomorrow or the day after tomorrow? Are you kidding me? All my stuff is in that suitcase!"

The clerk, clearly accustomed to such scenes, showed no surprise. "Don't worry, your luggage isn't lost forever. It'll arrive on the next flight from Frankfurt."

"And when is the next flight?"

"As I said—tomorrow, or perhaps the day after."

Tony felt his patience collapsing. "So you're saying I'm stuck here without luggage for two days?"

"You're not stuck. Your luggage will definitely be delivered. You may even receive compensation for your inconvenience," the clerk said, gesturing vaguely toward another desk.

Tony's temper flared. "You mean, because of this silly piece of paper, I have to waste my time and wait around indefinitely? I demand to see your manager!"

The clerk calmly raised his eyes, studying Tony closely. "Sir, you might make demands in America, but you're now in Ukraine. The complaints and suggestions book is currently with another administrator. Next!"

His tone reminded Tony precisely of the bored consul he'd met in Chicago.

"I demand an immediate meeting with your manager!" Tony repeated angrily.

"Come tomorrow around nine in the morning if you'd like," the clerk said dismissively. "Today's working hours are over. Nobody is available now."

It was pointless to argue further. Tony stepped away from the desk and walked slowly into the airport lobby, thinking about his next step.

Several cab drivers instantly approached, aggressively offering their services, but Tony waved them away irritably as if brushing off persistent flies.

Tony suddenly realized he was terribly hungry. As he glanced around the quiet terminal, he noticed a small café tucked away in the corner. He walked over and quickly ordered a hamburger and a cup of coffee. Out of habit, Tony reached into his jacket pocket for his credit card and froze. In a panic, he remembered that he'd stuffed the card, along with the travel agency's phone number, into his jacket back in Chicago—and now that jacket was lost somewhere along the way with his luggage.

He couldn't believe it. He had never been so careless before. Tony felt a fresh wave of irritation toward the Chicago airport clerk. If that damned clerk hadn't insisted on checking his bag, Tony would never have made such an amateurish mistake. He frantically shoved his hands into his pants pockets, desperately hoping to find something useful there. All he came up with was a handful of American dollars.

"We don't accept dollars!" snapped the cashier, a middle-aged woman with tightly pressed lips and pride in her voice, as if refusing foreign currency were a matter of national honor.

Tony looked around anxiously. It was late evening, and all the currency exchange booths were closed. He stood helplessly, his stomach rumbling angrily. Sighing heavily, he tried again, carefully placing the dollars on the counter and casting a pleading look at the cashier.

She stared at him skeptically for a moment, then reluctantly took the money as though doing Tony an enormous favor. He breathed a sigh of relief—at least he'd have something to eat.

But when he saw the receipt, his relief vanished instantly. Tony raised his eyebrows in shock. He stared at the printed numbers, mentally converting hryvnias into dollars and back again, unsure if he'd misunderstood.

The woman behind the cash register noticed his reaction and smirked slightly. "You don't like the prices? Feel free to exchange your dollars for hryvnias first and come back. I'm sure we'll still be open."

Tony shook his head, dismissing her sarcasm with a tired wave of his hand. He grabbed his food, found a seat at the nearest table, and sat down heavily. Picking up the small receipt again, he rechecked the numbers, feverishly recalculating in his head. With an exasperated sigh, he pushed the unfinished hamburger away in disgust, crumpled the receipt, and tossed it aside.

"And they say this country is poor," he muttered bitterly to himself. "With prices like this, Las Vegas looks like a discount store."

There was no point in staying at the airport, but Tony had nowhere else to go. He rose slowly from the table and made his way toward the exit.

Outside, the cold evening air sent shivers down his spine. Out of nowhere, a taxi pulled up next to him.

"Taxi? Kiev? Cheap ride!" called out the driver eagerly.

"How much?" Tony asked automatically.

"Do you have many bags?"

"Not even one."

The driver looked Tony over carefully. "Without bags, it's even cheaper. Only fifty U.S. dollars."

Tony pulled the remaining money from his pocket. After dinner, he had about eighty dollars left. "Thanks, but I'm not going anywhere."

The driver leaned forward slightly, sensing an opportunity slipping away. "Twenty, then—just for you. Only because I'm heading home, and Kiev is right on my way."

"How do you know it's on your way?" Tony replied skeptically.

Without waiting for an answer, Tony turned down the offer and slowly walked away from the airport, uncertain of where exactly he was headed. He stepped off the concrete path onto the grass as an airplane roared overhead. Somewhere in front of him lay an unfamiliar city he'd never visited. He was now in a strange country with foreign smells drifting through the air.

Tony stopped and looked up at the night sky, gazing at the stars glittering silently. No one was waiting for him in this country.

Once more, he asked himself what he should do next. Should he head toward the city?

Surprisingly, Tony felt neither despair, irritation, nor anxiety. In fact, he felt nothing at all, and that amazed him. Instead, a strange, soothing calm spread through him—a sense of comfort like a child who has just awakened from a bad dream, now safe in his mother's arms.

Instinctively, Tony bent down and scooped up a handful of earth. At that moment, the massive silhouette of another airplane passed swiftly above the trees behind him. For one fleeting yet vivid instant, Tony felt as though he had touched something incredibly significant, something that would forever alter the rest of his life.

A sudden, cold gust of wind snapped Tony back into reality. He was in a foreign country, without money, without belongings. Loneliness flooded over him, sharp and icy, piercing his heart.

Chapter 13

A group of young women emerged from the airport terminal, chatting cheerfully as they headed toward the minivan that regularly took them home after their shift. They'd just finished working the evening flight and were relieved that another long day had finally ended. Despite the late hour, they still looked fresh. They were the airport's unofficial attraction—bright, charming, and always friendly enough to make tired travelers smile.

Most of them were typical Ukrainian girls—young university students who balanced their studies with part-time work at the airport. The evening shift was always preferable: fewer travelers, no managers hovering around, and no early alarms ringing at dawn. On good days—and today was definitely a good day—they could even celebrate a little. Tonight was special: it was Tanya's birthday, which made the laughter louder and the mood brighter than usual.

Their shift had ended later than planned, and since buses didn't run at this hour, the girls relied on the minivan provided by the airport. As they approached their ride, one of them noticed a fellow standing alone near the edge of the parking lot, looking lost and uncertain. It was Tony, slowly making his way back toward the terminal.

"Hey girls, look—a man!" said Lena, the lively brunette with the bright red purse. She waved enthusiastically at Tony. "Hi!"

Tony didn't understand her Russian, but he waved back, grateful for any human interaction after the chaotic evening he'd had.

The girls laughed cheerfully at his response. "Look, he's not local," Lena giggled. Her friend Katya, dressed in a short skirt despite the evening chill, eyed Tony curiously. She noticed his stylish shirt, his high-quality jeans, and the expensive gold watch on his wrist. Clearly, he wasn't struggling financially.

Seeing their friendly faces, Tony walked over. Just moments ago, he'd felt completely isolated; now, he couldn't believe his luck at finding himself in such attractive company.

"Why are you alone, handsome?" Tanya asked playfully in surprisingly good English. She had soft, light-brown hair, warm eyes, and a voice that instantly made Tony relax.

"They lost me," Tony replied with a sheepish grin.

The girls laughed even louder. "Lost you? Are you a suitcase?" asked Katya cheerfully.

"The airline lost my suitcase," Tony explained, gesturing helplessly, "and while looking for it, I guess I got lost myself."

"Then call the people who were supposed to meet you," Tanya advised.

Tony shook his head, feeling a little embarrassed. "I can't. Their number's in my jacket—and my jacket's in my suitcase."

"So, what exactly are you waiting here for?" Lena asked, smiling. The other girls laughed again, clearly amused by Tony's predicament.

Suddenly, Lena's expression turned more serious. "Listen, handsome, there's no reason for you to stay here alone. Come with us to Kiev. By the way, it's Tanya's birthday," she said, nodding toward her friend. "And we're still missing a handsome guy like you to make the party perfect."

Tony hesitated. "I appreciate it, but... I don't have any money. My credit card was in the suitcase, and all I have is eighty dollars."

Lena waved off his concern with confidence. "Eighty dollars? That's plenty for wine and champagne. I already have candy and snacks at home. Come on!"

Before Tony could even respond, Lena gently took him by the arm, guiding him toward the waiting minivan. The other girls encouraged him cheerfully, their smiles irresistible. As the driver started the engine, Lena directed him to a late-night store to pick up drinks, happily spending Tony's remaining cash.

***

The party was in a cramped, dimly-lit apartment belonging to the girl with the red handbag. It was a tiny, one-room space perched on the top floor of a Soviet-era high-rise, overlooking the broad, mysterious Dnieper. The river gleamed faintly under the scattered moonlight, adding a haunting charm to the urban landscape outside the windows.

The shabby furniture, threadbare sofas, and worn-out chairs clashed strangely with the smooth oak parquet flooring beneath his feet. Back in the States, such expensive flooring was reserved for lavish homes, yet here it was paired with furnishings that would have seemed at home in a junkyard. This contrast intrigued him, stirring his curiosity as much as it unsettled him.

The hostess lit a candle, casting trembling shadows across the walls, and switched on some slow, sensual music. The soft notes filled the cramped room, mingling with whispers and the laughter of the girls who hurried to set the table. Soon, glasses sparkled under the dim candlelight as champagne bubbles glittered enticingly, capturing Tony's tired gaze.

After the exhausting journey, the loss of his belongings, and the emotional tension, Tony felt a warm wave of relaxation wash over him. The first sip of champagne loosened the knot of anxiety in his chest. By the time they'd finished the second bottle, he felt his thoughts drifting, blurred pleasantly by alcohol.

The girls drank with fervent enthusiasm, laughter becoming freer, their voices more flirtatious and uninhibited. Tony, swept up in the cheerful atmosphere, lost count of how many glasses he'd emptied, losing himself to the increasingly heated mood of the room.

An argument soon broke out playfully over who loved Tanya, the birthday girl, most of all. Giggling and teasing escalated until it was decided that the winner would be the one who kissed Tanya best.

"Tony, come on, show us what you've got!" Zhenya laughed, playfully pushing him towards Tanya. Her teasing voice held a challenge, daring him to cross a line he had not anticipated.

Tony hesitated for a heartbeat, aware suddenly of how his heart pounded in his chest. Tanya stood in front of him, cheeks flushed from alcohol, eyes glistening softly in the candlelight, full lips slightly parted. Tony briefly recalled Sofia, her image flickering into his mind, but the alcohol and jet lag blurred that thought into the shadows. A sudden wave of desire, reckless and electric, surged through him.

Slowly, Tony reached out, encircling Tanya's waist. Her body pressed softly into his embrace, warm and yielding. He leaned in, feeling her quickened breath brush against his lips as their mouths met. The kiss was tender, hesitant at first, but quickly intensified as Tanya responded eagerly, pressing against him, her pulse quickening in harmony with his own. Behind them, the girls laughed and applauded, breaking the spell.

"Tony, did they teach you nothing about kissing back in America?" Sveta teased, pushing him aside confidently. Tony collapsed into a chair, his lips still tingling, cheeks burning with a mixture of embarrassment and arousal.

Sveta, wearing her daringly short skirt, gently tilted Tanya's chin upward, her slender fingers brushing lightly across the girl's breast. Without hesitation, she captured Tanya's lips passionately, the intensity of the kiss silencing the room. Tony stared, mesmerized by the open passion, his pulse quickening as the girls' kiss became deeper and more urgent. When Sveta finally released Tanya, she threw Tony a triumphant look, her eyes sparkling mischievously.

Zhenya laughed softly, stepping forward with exaggerated confidence. "Sveta, you call that a kiss? Let me show you both how it's done properly," she whispered huskily.

Kneeling gracefully before Tanya, Zhenya moved with slow, deliberate seductiveness. In one smooth, practiced motion, she pulled Tanya's skirt upward, allowing her fingertips to trail teasingly along Tanya's trembling thighs. Gently, she hooked a finger beneath the delicate lace of Tanya's panties, carefully sliding them aside to reveal warm, bare skin glistening softly in the flickering candlelight. The room around them melted away, leaving only the warmth of their mingled breaths, the quiet pulse of music, and the intoxicating whispers of pleasure drifting gently through the darkness.

Tony's breath quickened sharply, his pulse still racing as Zhenya leaned closer. Her lips brushed Tanya's inner thighs, leaving a trail of heated kisses that climbed slowly upward, inch by agonizing inch. Tanya gasped, arching her back instinctively, her fingers tightening in Zhenya's hair as pleasure overtook her senses Tony felt himself lost in a swirl of erotic confusion, the boundaries of reality and fantasy rapidly dissolving. He sank deeper into this surreal, mesmerizing dance, unable to resist the alluring chaos around him.

Had Tony glanced out of the window at that very moment, past the silken shadows and flickering candlelight, he would have noticed the solemn golden domes of Kiev-Pechersk Monastery, glowing softly across the dark expanse of the Dnieper. But in that instant, he saw nothing but desire, heard nothing but the frantic beating of his heart, and felt nothing but the electrifying touch of strangers' skin.

Chapter 14

A sudden, shrill ringing sliced through the silence of the night. Groaning, Sasha rolled over and fumbled for his phone, squinting through sleepy eyes at the glowing screen. It was nearly four in the morning.

"Hello?" he muttered irritably.

An angry, strained voice barked into his ear. "Sasha, what the hell have you done with my wife?"

Still groggy, Sasha sat up, blinking in confusion. It took him a second to recognize the voice—it was Dima, Zhenya's husband. "Dima? What are you talking about? Hasn't Zhenya come home yet?"

"No, she hasn't!" Dima snapped back, his voice rising in panic and anger. "Tell me exactly where you took the girls after work!"

Sasha rubbed his face roughly with one hand, annoyance now mixing with his confusion. He had simply driven the airport crew—the girls from the evening shift—to the city, as always. Why was Dima shouting at him?

"Hey, calm down!" Sasha snapped. "I took them exactly where they told me, just like every night. They all went with some foreign guy. I dropped them off at Tanya's place. What's going on?"

"And where's Zhenya now?" Dima demanded sharply.

Sasha hesitated, suddenly feeling uneasy. "What do you mean, 'where'? She was with them, obviously. Where else would she go?"

***

Tanya reluctantly slipped out of bed, wrapping herself hastily in a robe as the persistent ringing of the doorbell grew louder and angrier. Tony barely registered the sound, his lips still locked onto Zhenya's neck, his consciousness clouded by alcohol and pleasure.

"Tanya, who the hell is it at this hour?" Svetka groaned irritably from the couch.

"Probably just the neighbors again," Tanya replied sleepily. "You know how they get when the music's too loud."

She shuffled to the front door, unfastened the chain with lazy annoyance, and turned the lock. But before she could open it fully, the door burst open violently, sending Tanya staggering back against the wall with a startled scream.

A tall, broad-shouldered man stood in the doorway, his face flushed with anger, eyes blazing with fury.

"Where the hell is Zhenya?" he roared, storming past Tanya into the apartment.

Tanya shrieked in panic, pressing herself against the wall. "Zhenya, your husband is here!"

Zhenya sat up abruptly in bed, her eyes wide with fear, instinctively clutching the bedsheet to her chest.

"Please, Dima, not my face!" she pleaded, shielding herself desperately. "I can't go to work with bruises again!"

Tony looked around in confusion, unable to understand a single word being shouted. Before he could react or speak, the angry husband lunged at him with a brutal punch that landed squarely on Tony's face, knocking him backward against the headboard. His vision blurred; stars exploded before his eyes.

"You bastard!" Dima shouted furiously. "Think you can come here and buy my wife with your filthy American money?"

Tony raised his hands defensively, blood beginning to drip from his nose. "Wait—stop! I don't know what you're—"

Another blow landed hard on his cheek, cutting off Tony's words with searing pain. Out of pure instinct, Tony blindly reached out, grabbing the nearest object—a half-empty champagne bottle from the bedside table—and swung it wildly, smashing it over the attacker's head. Glass shattered, scattering fragments everywhere. Blood trickled down Dima's forehead, mixing with the sweat and rage.

"You scratched me, you bastard!" Dima screamed, wiping blood from his brow. With a growl of renewed anger, he threw himself onto Tony, fists raining down with frightening force. Tony struggled desperately, kicking and pushing, trying to escape the onslaught.

"Stop it! Enough!" Tanya screamed, finally finding her voice. She and Zhenya desperately tried to pull the furious man away. The entire room was now filled with screams, shattered glass, and the metallic tang of blood.

Chapter 15

The sky outside was slowly turning gray, the first hints of morning breaking over the rooftops of the sleeping city. Tony sat hunched over on a hard plastic chair in the hospital emergency room, holding an ice pack to his swollen, aching face. Beside him, Sveta and Lena lounged casually, passing a beer bottle between them, their giggles breaking through the quiet tension of the waiting area.

A nurse gently cleaned the dried blood from Tony's forehead, her touch careful but brisk. He winced slightly as she pressed a gauze pad against the wound.

He glanced nervously at the girls, still not fully understanding how he'd ended up here.

"What'll happen to Zhenya?" Tony asked cautiously, his voice slightly muffled by his swollen lips.

"Zhenya? Nothing," Lena said lightly, taking a sip from the beer bottle. "She and Dima have been fighting their whole lives. They argue, make up, and then have great sex. They'll probably be curled up together by morning."

She leaned forward, examining Tony's injuries with exaggerated interest. "Wow, though. Dima really did a number on you. You're lucky he didn't throw you out of the window—he's a professional boxer, you know."

Sveta laughed softly, her voice tinged with envy and regret. "At least they still have passion," she muttered bitterly. "My husband is pathetic—last year, I gave him an STD, and he didn't even have the guts to slap me."

Lena burst into laughter. "Yeah, your husband's definitely no Dima. Or that handsome one from the airport," she added, nudging Tony playfully. "Look at his poor lips, so swollen. Listen," Lena said, switching to heavily accented English, "Tony, take us to America. Sveta and I will cook you real Ukrainian borscht. You've never tasted borscht like ours, full of vitamins—better than any medicine."

Both girls broke into laughter again, their voices echoing through the mostly empty waiting room. The nurse, who understood just enough English to follow along, shook her head, smiling softly despite herself.

At that moment, the heavy metal door at the end of the hallway creaked open. A sleepy-looking policeman, holding a worn folder, stepped into the corridor, glancing around impatiently.

"Where's the injured foreigner?" the officer called out, his voice gruff with irritation

"Oh, just what we needed," Lena muttered quietly to Sveta. "The police."

Sveta rolled her eyes and whispered back, "Where did he come from? As if we don't have enough problems already!"

Lena shrugged, nodding subtly towards the nurse. "They have to report these kinds of things."

Then, quickly returning to English, Lena patted Tony's shoulder comfortingly. "Don't worry, handsome. Your wounds aren't fatal. You'll heal. And besides, scars make men even sexier. Remember, we didn't abandon you—we brought you here. Right, Sveta?"

Sveta nodded in exaggerated seriousness. "We have to go now," she said to Tony, touching his hand lightly as they stood. "We've got work soon."

Tony waved weakly as the two girls made their way toward the door, still laughing quietly. As they exited, the policeman stepped heavily into the waiting room, eyeing Tony with suspicion as he approached.

***

Tony sat slumped on an uncomfortable wooden chair in the police station, looking hopelessly around the shabby office. His head still throbbed beneath the fresh bandages, and a faint smell of antiseptic lingered around him. Above his head hung a faded sign with bold Cyrillic letters, which, if he had been able to read Russian, would have informed him solemnly: "Uniting all our forces to fight criminals." But to Tony, these strange letters might as well have been ancient hieroglyphs.

The police officers in the station glanced at him now and then, shrugging and shaking their heads as if Tony were some strange animal whose origin they could not determine. Nobody here spoke English, and Tony had given up trying to communicate.

Each attempt to explain himself had ended with confused silence or irritated gestures.

Finally, the chief appeared, a stocky man with heavy bags under his eyes and a weary expression. After a brief, hushed conversation with the other policemen, he summoned an officer who claimed to have studied English at school.

The officer—young and visibly nervous—stood before Tony, cleared his throat loudly, and, after a long pause, uttered politely: "How do you do?"

Tony stared back at him, exhausted and incredulous.

The chief turned angrily to the officer. "Is that all you can say? How the hell did you get good grades in English?"

The younger officer flushed, muttered something unintelligible, and stepped back, relieved to disappear from the spotlight.

The chief sighed and began pacing restlessly back and forth, rubbing his forehead. Another policeman seated nearby cautiously asked, "So what do we do with him now?"

"How should I know?" the chief snapped irritably. "We don't want him hanging around here. The last thing we need is some international incident. Why did you even bring him here in the first place?"

The officer looked puzzled. "What else was I supposed to do— leave him lying in the street?"

The chief groaned. "What did he have on him besides his passport and tickets?"

"Two dollars, a wristwatch, and a handkerchief."

"Hmm." The chief rubbed his chin thoughtfully. "Did he file a complaint against anyone?"

"No, he just wants out of here as soon as possible." The policeman grinned a little at Tony's forlorn figure. "Poor guy keeps repeating two words like a broken record—'airplane' and 'Boryspil.'"

The chief frowned. "And what about the girls who were with him? Those two prostitutes?"

The officer shrugged. "Who knows where they went? Probably home."

"And you didn't get their names, their addresses—nothing? What kind of policeman are you?"

The officer took off his cap and scratched his head, embarrassed. "How was I supposed to know we'd need that?"

The chief sighed again deeply, glancing at Tony with genuine frustration. "This whole situation could seriously ruin our statistics."

The young policeman eagerly put his cap back on. "Maybe we should just drop him off at the airport? He might recognize someone there. Maybe he fell behind his tourist group or something."

The chief considered this for a moment, then nodded resignedly. "Fine, take him to Boryspil. Get him out of our hair."

The officer beckoned impatiently to Tony. With growing unease, Tony stood up and obediently followed the policeman. As they left the building, he suddenly felt cold panic rising in his chest. Where were they taking him? Maybe somewhere outside the city to get rid of him without witnesses? Tony recalled with horror the stories he'd read online about corrupt foreign police, disappearances, and tourists never heard from again.

The chief watched Tony's departure and shook his head, muttering to himself, "And they say America is a beacon of democracy! Here's your democracy—right here in front of our eyes. This guy barely steps off the plane, gets drunk in our Slavic tradition, and jumps straight into bed with the first whores he finds. Now he can't even remember where he left his bags. And they claim to have freedom! Nonsense. With us, people at least know how to relax and enjoy real freedom without the constant fear of lawsuits and scandals."

Chapter 16

Tony's lost luggage arrived exactly as promised on the very next flight. When the police dropped him off at the airport, his suitcase and bag were already waiting near the reception desk, looking as innocent as if they'd never caused him trouble at all.

"You see? Nothing happened to your luggage." The woman behind the counter gave Tony's bruised and swollen face a curious glance. "And you were worried!"

Tony didn't reply. Silently, he grabbed his things, stepped aside, and unzipped his bag with trembling hands. He let out a deep sigh of relief when he found his jacket right where he'd left it. Reaching into the pocket, Tony closed his eyes briefly, praying. His credit card and the tourist agency's phone numbers were there, safe and sound.

Trying to control his shaking fingers, Tony walked to the nearest payphone and dialed the first number on the list. Anxiety surged through him as he listened to the distant ring. What if no one there spoke English? What if he couldn't communicate what had happened?

A woman answered, her voice deep and weary. Tony had barely begun explaining his situation when she interrupted him, switching abruptly into hesitant but understandable English.

"We've been waiting for you since yesterday," she said slowly. "Please stay in the airport. Our representative will pick you up shortly—in about forty minutes."

Her words, though simple, felt like a lifesaver thrown to a drowning man. Tony leaned against the payphone, breathing deeply, suddenly grateful that someone in this foreign country knew he existed. He felt less alone.

As he waited, Tony watched the people passing by. Some hurried, pushing carts loaded with luggage; others strolled aimlessly, killing time before flights. A young woman stood just a few feet away, tears streaming down her face as she clung to her boyfriend. Tony found himself wondering about them—was it just a short goodbye, or was this the end of their story? Watching this small drama unfold, he realized he was seeing fragments of strangers' lives, brief scenes that would remain forever incomplete.

The last twenty-four hours had shaken Tony in a way nothing ever had before. In America, he'd always played by the rules. He'd never even set foot in a police station; much less been arrested. Now, his mind kept replaying his experience in the Ukrainian police station, and he was haunted by unanswered questions. Had he officially been arrested? Would it affect his record? Could it damage his career?

The unknown gnawed at him. Tony couldn't possibly have imagined that the police officers had breathed sighs of relief as soon as they dropped him off. There were no reports, no paperwork, nothing to indicate he'd ever been there. But ignorance didn't comfort Tony. His mind conjured terrifying scenarios of being arrested upon returning to Chicago, of being accused of solicitation, of seeing his career and life unravel in court.

His thoughts spiraled even further. His ribs ached sharply; his head throbbed from either the blows or the alcohol—he wasn't even sure which anymore.

Tony tried to recall the last time he'd fought. Despite his difficult personality, he'd never physically fought anyone—not even as a kid. The prestigious school he attended had zero tolerance for violence. Screaming and swearing were fine, but one touch and you'd be expelled instantly. Yet, here he was, bruised and battered from his first real fight.

Then Sofia entered his mind like a ghost, bringing another wave of guilt and fear. Tony had never intended to be loyal, but somehow, with Sofia, it had just naturally happened. He hadn't wanted anyone else since meeting her. But last night, he'd broken that without even realizing what he was doing—and with multiple women. The thought struck him cold: AIDS. Tony wiped sudden beads of cold sweat from his forehead. Ukraine was notorious for its HIV statistics, and he hadn't bothered with protection. If he'd caught something, it wouldn't just end his career—it would end everything. He'd return home in a coffin instead of with his grandfather's handful of earth.

Tony shook his head vigorously, desperately pushing the horrifying thoughts aside. It couldn't end this way. He refused to believe his destiny could unravel so absurdly. His life had a purpose, and he hadn't fulfilled it yet.

Until now, Tony had always believed his career was the foundation of his happiness. With enough money and professional success, everything else would effortlessly fall into place—at least, that's what he had always told himself. And he was damn good at what he did. One of America's top specialists in flight data recorder systems, he had worked on classified projects and was trusted implicitly with highly sensitive government contracts. But for the first time, Tony was beginning to question whether being at the top of his field truly meant anything.

Suddenly, an even darker thought gripped him. What if yesterday's disaster had been deliberately staged? Could it be the KGB setting him up? He laughed bitterly at himself—there was no KGB anymore; it had vanished with the Soviet Union. Yet the paranoid thought refused to fully fade away.

Fragments of last night surged chaotically through Tony's mind: laughter, glasses clinking, tangled limbs, and faces blurred by alcohol. Then came the police station's oppressive atmosphere, the frustration of lost luggage, and confusion. Tony felt overwhelmed, dizzy, and utterly helpless.

But suddenly, amidst this chaos, one clear memory surfaced. He recalled stepping outside the airport for the first time and feeling the Ukrainian earth between his fingers. With stunning clarity, he remembered the surprising peace he'd felt at that moment. It was as if his grandfather had stood right beside him, placing a comforting hand on his shoulder. The sensation of his grandfather's presence was so strong that Tony turned instinctively, glancing behind him.

"Tony?" a voice startled him back to reality. A young man holding a sign labeled "Interterm" approached quickly, smiling apologetically. "We've been waiting for you since yesterday. Why didn't you inform us about your delay? We would have come immediately."

Tony didn't feel like explaining. Instead, he allowed the representative to take his luggage and guide him to the waiting car.

He settled into the comfortable back seat and finally relaxed, watching the Ukrainian landscape glide past through the window. Though he'd technically visited the city already, only now, in daylight, did Tony truly see Kiev.

The representative chatted amiably, pointing out various landmarks and handing Tony glossy brochures. Tony nodded politely, but inwardly, he wished only for solitude. He longed for a quiet hotel room, a hot bath, and sleep—most of all, sleep.

As if reading his mind, the representative smiled gently and offered to meet him again in the morning to organize a proper city tour. Tony agreed absently, turning back toward the window.

Chapter 17

Tony opened his eyes. For a moment, he had no idea where he was or how he had gotten there. The darkness around him felt dense and unfamiliar, and the strange smells in the air didn't match the scents of home. The sheets beneath him felt rougher than usual, the mattress somehow firmer. A soft, distant hum of cars whispered through the window, deepening his sense of disorientation.

He propped himself up on his elbows, attempting to sit up, and immediately groaned in pain. Every movement sent a throbbing pulse through his aching body. He reached up gingerly to touch his swollen jaw, instantly remembering the previous night—the fight, the unfamiliar apartment, the strange people whose faces he could barely recall. A wave of unease washed over him.

Tony sat up carefully, swung his legs off the bed, and glanced toward the window. Outside, an unfamiliar city lay sleeping beneath pale predawn skies. Grayish-blue shadows outlined buildings he had never seen before, structures whose names and histories he didn't yet know. He realized he had collapsed onto the bed before without even taking off his clothes or washing away the dust and grime of travel. Now he felt dirty and bruised, unsettled not only physically but emotionally as well.

Feeling around in the semi-darkness, he finally found the bedside lamp and flicked it on. A dull yellow glow illuminated the hotel room, revealing furniture. He looked for his watch, something he always placed carefully beside the bed, but it wasn't on the nightstand. Puzzled and annoyed, Tony wondered briefly if someone had entered while he slept and stolen it.

He squinted at the hotel clock on the table. Five o'clock in the morning. It's too early for any sense of normalcy. Sighing, Tony stood, grimacing slightly from the pain. His fingers absently ran along his wrist—and there was his watch, securely fastened in place. For the first time he could recall, he'd slept without removing it.

Removing the watch and setting it down on the bathroom sink, Tony turned on the shower. As the water warmed, he studied his reflection in the mirror. The face staring back at him seemed like someone else's, battered, bruised, with dark circles beneath weary eyes. Tony shook his head slowly, barely recognizing the man he'd become in just one day.

Stepping into the shower, he shivered at the initial coolness. Gradually, warm water soothed his aching muscles, washing away the tension and confusion. As water streamed down his body, Tony tried to organize his thoughts. What should he do now? Go back to bed? Explore the hotel? He had always been so careful, so organized; even his vacations were meticulously planned. Now, here he was—in a strange country, caught in chaos, improvising every step of the way. Nothing was going according to his carefully designed plans. The realization both frightened and intrigued him.

Emerging from the shower, Tony dressed slowly, deliberately, as if each piece of clothing could restore his sense of order. He glanced briefly around the empty hotel room, considered returning to bed, then quickly dismissed the idea. Sleep was out of the question; his mind was restless, still racing with unfamiliar anxieties and doubts. Tony stepped out of the room into the silent hotel hallway, feeling an urge to escape the loneliness.

He passed the empty reception desk, where two bored-looking prostitutes watched him listlessly. Ignoring them, Tony followed the sharp aroma of alcohol and cigars toward the sound of muffled laughter and music. He found the hotel bar crowded despite the late hour. Loud voices and heavy laughter filled the room, the air thick with cigarette smoke and alcohol.

Tony squeezed through the crowd, leaning heavily against the polished bar.

"Coffee! A cup of coffee!" he shouted to the bartender, struggling to be heard over the thumping bass and the laughter around him.

A sudden shove nearly knocked him off balance.

"Oh, sorry there, partner," said a middle-aged man dressed like a cowboy, staggering heavily. His hat dangled loosely from his hand. Tony stared at him in confusion—this stranger had spoken first in Russian, then immediately switched to English, heavily accented but unmistakably American.

"No worries," Tony muttered automatically, trying to steady himself.

The cowboy grinned broadly, immediately grabbing Tony by the shoulders with drunken enthusiasm. "Well, I'll be damned! Are you an American, too?"

Tony smiled weakly, unexpectedly relieved to hear English again. "Yes, I'm from Chicago."

"Chicago! The land of Al Capone!" laughed the cowboy boisterously, drawing curious glances from nearby patrons. "I'm from Texas myself. Been here for seven years. Finest country in the world! And the women..." He whistled appreciatively, winking at Tony.

Tony stared at the stranger in disbelief. "Seven years? How can you possibly live here? Isn't the economy terrible?"

"Economy? Ha!" the cowboy scoffed loudly, slapping Tony amicably on the shoulder. "Buddy, the economy here is only bad for people who lack imagination. Trust me, friend, for every dollar I invest in Ukraine, I make five! This place is a gold mine. We're sittin' right over there," he said, pointing vaguely toward a corner table crowded with giggling women.

Tony watched him stumble away through the crowd, confused and troubled by the cowboy's casual boast. Were those drunken exaggerations, or was there truth behind his words? Tony finished his coffee quickly, feeling a growing pressure in his temples from the noise and smoke. He stepped out of the bar into the empty, echoing lobby and walked outside.

The crisp morning air immediately cleared his head. Tony strolled slowly down the unfamiliar streets, watching as the city slowly awoke. He noted absently the lack of diversity around him—no African Americans, no Asians, only pale, tired faces rushing to unknown jobs and destinations.

The cowboy's words returned again and again, echoing inside his mind. Five dollars for every dollar invested—was such a thing possible here? If so, why did this country look so worn, tired, and poor?

A sudden, sharp loneliness pierced him deeply. Tony stopped abruptly, feeling as if the whole world had grown darker and colder around him. For the first time, he genuinely regretted leaving Sofia behind. He wished desperately she was here, by his side. The emptiness of the streets mirrored the emptiness he felt inside. He imagined what it would be like to have a home, a family, someone who waited for him at the end of each journey.

Almost without thinking, he returned swiftly to his hotel room, picked up the phone, and dialed the familiar number. Her voice on the other end brought a painful joy flooding into his heart.

"Tony, dear, is everything all right?" Sofia's voice trembled slightly. "Why didn't you call sooner? I was so worried..."

"I couldn't call. I..." He hesitated, embarrassed by his own confusion. "I was busy, Sofia. I'm sorry."

She sighed gently. "It's okay. Are you well?"

"Everything's fine. How are things there?" He tried to smile, but his voice betrayed his fatigue.

"I'm fine. What's Ukraine like?"

Tony glanced out the window. The sunrise now bathed the unfamiliar city in a soft golden glow. "Different," he said simply.

She laughed gently. "Like another planet?"

"Something like that," he replied quietly, still gazing at the horizon. His heart ached as she whispered softly into the phone, "Come home soon, Tony. I miss you."

He didn't answer, merely holding the phone tighter, silently watching the sun rise over the strange city.

Chapter 18

Tony stepped into the hotel lobby, still feeling the lingering buzz of fatigue and adrenaline from the last few days. He spotted the travel agency representative hunched over a table, idly flipping through a pile of glossy pamphlets. At Tony's approach, the man's expression lit up with sudden interest, as if he'd spotted the winning ticket in a raffle.

"I've gathered quite a range for you," the representative said, sliding a stack of brochures bound by a flimsy paper clip across the table. "These are our recommended tours. Don't assume picking them individually will be cheaper—our company's package deals often save you money."

Tony took the brochures, giving the vibrant photos and punchy slogans only a passing glance. His mind was drifting elsewhere. "Thanks," he mumbled, laying them down again. "I'll look them over and let you know if I decide on something." Then he paused, eyeing the representative more carefully. "By the way…did I hear right that returns on investments can be pretty high around here?"

That question lit a spark in the representative's eyes. He straightened in his chair as though he'd sensed a real opportunity. Tony recognized the expression—it reminded him of when he was back in the States, whenever talk turned to promising ventures.

"Yes, exactly. It's one of those golden moments," the man explained, his English slipping slightly in his enthusiasm. "Ukraine is going through changes—think of it as an untamed frontier, the way America was in the days of the Wild West. Your country has everything pinned down with regulations, but here, it's wide open. If you're thinking of investing, you couldn't pick a better time."

Tony shifted his weight, letting the possibility linger. "Maybe," he said, speaking with a cautious tone, although part of him felt a tingle of curiosity. He had always toyed with the idea of building something for himself instead of funneling his energy into someone else's project.

"That's great!" The representative beamed, tapping the brochures for emphasis. "I have friends—very capable businesspeople. I'd be happy to arrange a meeting."

The thought stirred a flicker of excitement in Tony. He'd never followed through on his entrepreneurial ideas, but maybe now, in this strange place, it was worth exploring. "Sure," he replied. "I'll at least hear them out."

"Excellent." The man nodded eagerly. "As for these tours—anything catches your eye?"

"I'll call if that changes," Tony said. He'd already decided on his own itinerary: a visit to the Kiev-Pechersk Monastery.

"Understood." The representative smoothed out a crease on one of the pamphlets, then smiled politely. "And if you need anything else, including that business introduction, I'm just a phone call away. We can set it up anytime."

Tony thanked him, scooped up the brochures, and headed toward the lobby doors. As he walked, he realized that underneath all the recent chaos—lost luggage, unexpected brawls, and sleepless nights—he felt an unfamiliar buzz of anticipation. Maybe there was more to this country than disorganized encounters and chaotic nights. The idea of stepping into unknown territory, both in business and life, sent a small thrill coursing through him, a spark of excitement he rarely allowed himself to feel.

***

Tony stepped into the dimly lit "Department for Tourists" area, only to find a bored-looking woman with her nose buried in a worn paperback novel. The small sign above her head felt incongruously official for such a casual setting. He cleared his throat softly.

"May I order an individual tour here?" he asked.

She looked up, and Tony noticed the faint surprise flicker behind her tired eyes. "Sure, why not. But you'll have to wait until one of our girls is free." Her English was surprisingly fluent, though tinged with a slight accent.

"That's fine." Tony watched her change his money for a simple paper ticket. "I'm not in a hurry."

"Then wait by the entrance. They'll come for you," she instructed, offering him only a fleeting glance before turning back to her book.

Tony stepped outside into the monastery courtyard, mildly irritated that this sacred place felt so ordinary. He'd expected something profound—an almost mystical revelation the moment he passed through the gates. Instead, he found the typical bustle of tourists and the mundane exchange of money for services.

A small ripple of disappointment tugged at him. He'd journeyed here much like a pilgrim in the Middle Ages traveling on foot to Jerusalem—his heart thundering with anticipation as he'd first glimpsed the Monastery's ancient walls. This was, after all, the very place his grandfather's will had pointed him toward, a place that was supposed to hold some cryptic secret, some sacred meaning. Yet everything he saw seemed only dusty, everyday reality.

He briefly considered leaving altogether. Maybe the will had no hidden clues, no deeper significance. Returning to Chicago on the earliest flight suddenly felt like the smartest choice.

A sudden voice interrupted his thoughts. "Did you order an individual tour?"

Tony turned to find a delicate-looking girl with strikingly large brown eyes. Her long, dark hair was pinned neatly into a bun, and despite her fragile appearance, she seemed poised and self-assured.

"Yes," he answered, finding himself unexpectedly charmed by her presence. She looked like a young woman who had somehow retained the innocent grace of a child.

"I'm Vera." She extended her hand with a gentle smile. "I'll be telling you about this monastery."

Her tone was soft, yet it seemed to carry the weight of ancient secrets. With an effortless motion, she led Tony indoors, moving as though a gentle breeze guided her steps.

"Please, don't be put off by how simple it looks," she murmured as if reading the doubt on Tony's face. "Try not to focus on outward appearances—look for the spirit of the saints. Kiev-Pechersk Monastery, or the Monastery of the Kiev Caves, is truly one of the world's wonders. It's home to twenty-two churches. The architectural complex is on UNESCO's list of valuable monuments."

She spoke calmly, her voice carrying a hypnotic rhythm that Tony found strangely soothing. "During Soviet times, much of the Monastery's purpose was suppressed. The regime insisted that religion was unnecessary. They tried turning this sacred place into a museum. Their goal was to break the spirit and faith of the Ukrainian people. But they couldn't do it—this place, and the nation, survived."

Her words stirred something in Tony. It was as if her voice reached inside and lightly tugged at his heart, dissolving his earlier irritation. Slowly, their conversation transformed from a standard tour guide's monologue into a quiet, intimate dialogue. Tony felt an inexplicable lightness with this girl by his side. She led him through the Holy Trinity Church, its golden domes blazing under the mid-morning sun, and on toward the Near Caves, where Saint Antony was said to be entombed.

The Kiev Pechersk Lavra crowned the city's highest hill, its golden domes seeming to stretch upward in search of the heavens. Anyone crossing onto its territory felt as though they'd been transported into a much older era. Narrow roads of worn yellow bricks twisted past Byzantine-inspired structures, inviting visitors to slow down and reflect. On weekdays, the entire site was serene, broken only by the whispers of curious visitors and the distant hum of the city.

Monks rarely emerged, allowing tour guides to escort guests through various points of interest. One section of the Monastery had indeed become a museum, while another remained an active place of worship. People came in droves—not just for the remarkable beauty but for spiritual solace, to attend services, or to pray. Despite all the changes over centuries, the Monastery's essence hadn't been diminished. It clung to its sanctity, refusing to be stripped of its quiet, unbreakable soul.

"You mentioned relics of the saints," Tony said as they started down the cool stone steps into the dimly lit caves. "Is that where Saint Antony's remains are?"

Vera nodded politely, tucking a loose strand of hair back into her bun. "His relics are here, but no one has ever seen them. According to his will, after his death, no eyes were to gaze upon his body. The monks followed his wishes exactly. In the last years of his life, he rarely left his cave. After he passed away, they sealed it, and nobody saw him again. That's what the ancient chronicles say."

"A thousand years," Tony murmured, his voice echoing softly through the tunnel. "That's how long it's been since then…"

"When you're in these caves, it feels like everything happened only yesterday," Vera said quietly.

A wave of unease washed over Tony, making his heart lurch. "Strange," he whispered, wiping a thin bead of sweat from his forehead. "No one's tried opening the grave all this time?"

"Apparently not," Vera replied with a delicate shrug. "Communists had other things on their minds, and the monks never needed physical proof to believe. There was a rumor about some attempt, though. Word is that once they started to break the seal, water flooded in from nowhere, even though that part of the cave was bone-dry. They took it as a sign from above and stopped."

"What about the people who tried?" Tony asked, feeling a chill creep along his spine.

"They say it ended badly for them," Vera replied, her eyes flickering with concern. "I'm not sure about the details, but if you want, I can try to find out more."

She studied Tony curiously. Most tourists didn't ask such pointed, anxious questions about sealed tombs and invisible remains. Together, they joined a small group of pilgrims entering one of the narrower caverns. A single candle illuminated the space, revealing centuries-old icons and rough, earthen walls.

Tony paused before the icon dedicated to Saint Antony, its painted eyes solemn and deep. "It's odd," he said. "I feel like I've seen those eyes before…like that exact expression."

Vera's gaze followed his. Her voice went hushed, almost reverent. "This place has a powerful energy. There are only a few spots like this in the entire world. People say they sometimes hear things they can't explain."

Tony turned to her, his emotions swirling in confusion and curiosity. "You really believe that?"

"And you don't?" she countered simply.

Their eyes locked for a moment, the candle's flame flickering between them in a faint draft. A dark shadow seemed to sweep past the icon of Saint Antony, so close it nearly touched them both.

Chapter 19

"How did you become a tour guide?" Tony asked Vera, gently holding her elbow as they slowly made their way uphill along the winding brick roads leading away from the monastery.

She glanced at him sideways, a faint smile playing on her lips as if recalling something pleasant. "It wasn't difficult, really. History has always fascinated me." She tucked a stray lock of her dark hair behind her ear, her eyes glowing softly. "At the university, I wrote my thesis about Kiev-Pechersk Monastery. After spending so much time studying its past, it seemed natural to stay here. My older brother helped me get this job."

Tony felt her excitement quietly radiating from each word. "He works here too?"

"No," she shook her head lightly, the movement delicate yet certain. "He's in construction. But the monastery—it's his passion. He dreams of restoring it completely. Did you know," she said, suddenly animated, her brown eyes brightening even more, "the monastery used to occupy twice the territory it does today? This street in front of us, now called Sichnevoho Povstannia, wasn't here back then. It appeared much later."

Vera spoke eagerly, waving her slender hand as if trying to reconstruct the past in midair. Tony couldn't help but be drawn in by her enthusiasm. He watched her gestures, graceful and vivid, almost childlike in their purity, yet hiding a womanly seriousness beneath.

"In the late eighteenth century, when Catherine the Great visited Kiev, she looked around in surprise and asked, 'But where's the city?' Back then, Kiev was divided into three distinct parts," Vera continued, counting each one off on her slender fingers. "Podol, the district near the river, was filled with artisans and merchants; the upper city—Reign Town—where noblemen and wealthy citizens lived; and here, Kiev-Pechersk Monastery, a spiritual center bustling with monks, pilgrims, and scholars."

As they walked, groups of tourists passed by in waves, their whispers blending with the rhythmic toll of monastery bells drifting on the warm breeze. The air was filled with the faint, sweet aroma of burning incense, mingling gently with the scent of blooming lilacs from the monastery gardens. The path was shaded by tall trees, casting cool, lace-like shadows onto the ancient yellow bricks beneath their feet.

Tony felt as if they walked in a timeless sanctuary, far removed from the loud city streets he had seen only hours before. The contrast was striking. Outside the monastery gates, traffic rushed endlessly past grey Soviet-era apartment blocks and noisy construction sites. Here, each stone held centuries of calm, the ancient walls painted in faded white and soft gold, the smooth textures hinting at countless restorations over the years.

"It's strange, isn't it?" Tony spoke softly, almost to himself. "You walk through those gates, and suddenly you're in another world. It's as if time froze here, centuries ago."

Vera stopped briefly, turning toward him with her eyes glowing warmly, touched by his observation. "Exactly!" she said with quiet joy. "This place has its own heartbeat. I always feel that history is not just something written in old books. It's alive here, in every tree, in every brick, in every sound."

Tony smiled softly at her passionate words. He noticed how her cheeks reddened slightly as she spoke, and how her eyes sparkled with enthusiasm. He liked seeing this side of her— open, sincere, unguarded. It made her even more beautiful to him.

"Don't you sometimes feel," Vera continued thoughtfully, lowering her voice as if sharing a secret, "that modern life moves too fast? Everything changes overnight. But here, here at the monastery, you can breathe freely, you can pause and think."

She glanced upward, eyes tracing the golden domes gleaming against the sky, and Tony followed her gaze. Above them, the monastery rose majestically, its domes and towers shimmering gently in the sun. He thought about Vera's words, felt their truth resonating deeply within himself.

"Yes," Tony said finally, breaking the quiet pause. "This place gives you the time you need to understand what's really important."

Vera's eyes met his, reflecting a warmth and understanding he hadn't expected. Her gaze lingered for a moment, gentle and curious, before she shyly lowered her lashes and smiled. They stood in comfortable silence, letting the atmosphere of the monastery envelop them completely.

At last, they moved forward again, slowly emerging from the monastery gates back into the city. As soon as they stepped outside, the familiar noise of traffic. Tony blinked, momentarily disoriented by the abrupt transition.

For a second, he looked back at the monastery's walls, feeling an unexpected pang of longing, as though he'd left something meaningful behind.

Vera noticed his hesitation. "It's always a bit strange to return to the real world, isn't it?" she asked softly, reading his thoughts.

Tony nodded slowly, glancing back at her. "It's like stepping out of a beautiful dream."

"Exactly." Vera smiled, her expression warm yet tinged with a subtle sadness. "But now that you've experienced it, you can carry it with you wherever you go."

***

At the same time, in a luxurious office on the top floor of a high-rise in the city center, a representative from a travel agency nervously perched on the edge of a leather sofa. Across from him, in a massive leather armchair, sat a powerful man in an impeccably tailored, expensive pinstripe suit. Thick gold cufflinks gleamed on his sleeves, and on the polished oak desk between them lay a heavy antique writing instrument. The scent of tobacco and leather lingered in the air.

"How can you be so sure this American has money?" the man asked slowly in a deep, low voice, quiet yet unmistakably authoritative. His sharp eyes narrowed, carefully studying his guest's face, as if trying to read his hidden thoughts.

The travel agent leaned forward slightly, eager to convince him. "You should've seen how much he spent just for this trip to Ukraine! He took the most expensive suite at the hotel—overlooking the Dnieper—and didn't even blink when he saw the price. He's got a solid gold Rolex on his wrist. And the way he dresses…"

The expression on the large man's face remained unchanged. He slowly pulled a cigar from a carved mahogany box, carefully clipped the tip with practiced precision, struck a match, and brought it to the end. For a few moments, he smoked in silence, thinking over the agent's words.

"So he's rich," he finally said, letting out a thin stream of blue smoke. "But does he have any real interest in investing, or is he just sightseeing?"

The agent leaned closer, dropping his voice confidentially, as if afraid someone else might overhear. "He's interested, believe me. Definitely interested. He asked questions himself. You know how Americans are—they come to Eastern Europe sniffing around, looking for easy money. I suggested arranging a meeting, and he didn't refuse. He seemed intrigued."

The large man nodded thoughtfully, gazing into the distance. His fingertips tapped rhythmically on the polished desk.

"All right," he said calmly, yet with an underlying threat. "Arrange the meeting. But understand this clearly: if this American turns out to be a waste of our time, you'll personally answer for it."

The travel agent swallowed nervously, his throat suddenly dry. "He's the real deal, trust me. You won't regret it."

"I never regret," the man replied calmly, setting aside his cigar and looking directly into the agent's eyes. A faint but unmistakably dangerous smile flickered across his lips. "Arrange everything. Soon."

***

Tony walked along the street, listening closely to Vera.

"In the period I'm telling you about, Kiev was a border town. The boundary with Poland ran just thirty kilometers from the city limits. Peter the Great needed a strong fortress, and the monastery grounds were perfect for that. That's why he built an earthen rampart exactly where the Motherland Monument and the Square of Glory stand today."

Vera gestured toward the street ahead. "The road we're walking along now divides the Kiev-Pechersk Monastery into two parts. Despite protests from the monks, Peter garrisoned his soldiers here, moving troops from the northern provinces of the Russian Empire into Kiev. But soldiers and monks have completely different lifestyles, so a massive wall was built on both sides of the monastery entrance."

Tony glanced curiously to his right. "What's on the other side today?"

"It's still a military area, but there's a plan to restore that part of the monastery entirely," Vera answered.

Tony smiled skeptically. "Do you really think that's possible? Such a huge project would cost a fortune."

Vera shrugged gently. "Maybe. It's hard to explain to someone who isn't from here."

"No, I get it," Tony reassured her softly. "I really do understand. By the way, what's that monument over there?"

"I mentioned it already," Vera smiled patiently. "That's the Motherland Monument. It was built during Soviet times. Inside, there's a museum dedicated to World War II."

"Can you go up to the top?" Tony asked with interest.

"I think so. Honestly, I haven't been up there myself for a very long time. There's an observation deck at the top, and as long as the monument still stands, people can visit it."

Tony raised his eyebrows. "What do you mean, 'as long as it stands'?"

"Well, the Motherland Monument doesn't really belong here. Just as Jerusalem is a spiritual center for three religions— Judaism, Islam, and Christianity—Kiev is considered the capital of the Slavic Orthodox world. Here, a sword shouldn't rise higher than the cross," Vera explained.

"How long has it been standing there?"

"Since 1981," said Vera thoughtfully.

Tony let out a low whistle. "Wow. That's quite a while."

Vera laughed softly, shaking her head. "Quite a while? Twenty or twenty-five years is only a moment in history."

"You really think they'll tear it down?" Tony asked skeptically.

"I think so," she replied.

Tony shook his head slowly. "I don't get it. It doesn't bother anyone, does it? What's the point in destroying history?" He looked thoughtfully up at the massive figure looming above them. "It doesn't seem right to me. The monument represents a part of Ukrainian history. If you tear out pages from your history book, you risk losing something valuable."

Vera looked at Tony in genuine surprise. "I didn't expect to hear that from someone like you."

Tony laughed softly. "Honestly, neither did I. I was just thinking out loud."

Vera smiled, and they both fell into a comfortable silence for a moment.

Tony glanced upward again. "Why didn't the monks build anything on that hill? Was there something else up there before?"

"Since ancient times, that hill has been considered cursed. It's known as the Devil's Mountain. That's why no one ever built there. From a geological standpoint, the hill is made up of shifting sediment layers that are constantly moving. But the Communists ignored the geology. Now, every year they have to reinforce the hill so that the lady with the sword doesn't slide down into the Dnieper," Vera explained, smiling slightly.

They reached a bus stop, and Vera paused. "This is my stop."

Tony looked around in confusion, then back at Vera. "Thank you for today. That was honestly the most interesting tour of my life."

He stopped speaking abruptly, catching Vera's eyes. "Can I call you sometime?"

"Why?" Vera asked quietly, meeting his gaze.

"I want to see you again," Tony admitted softly.

"You can come back to the monastery anytime," she suggested lightly.

"I don't have much time left here." Tony hesitated, then continued with unexpected openness. "I haven't felt the way I feel with you for a long time. I don't know what it means or why it's happening, but I need to see you again."

Then, almost in a whisper, he added, "I'm telling you the truth."

Vera tilted her head slightly, observing him carefully, as if trying to see beneath his words. Finally she said, "Write down my phone number."

The bus was approaching. Tony searched his pockets and hastily pulled out the old monastery map to write on. Vera handed him a pen, watching curiously as he scribbled down her number.

"Wait—is that an old map of Kiev-Pechersk Monastery? I thought I knew almost everything about this place. I've seen many old maps, but never this one." She leaned closer, studying it with keen interest. "Where did you get this?"

"I brought it from Chicago," Tony replied with a gentle smile.

Vera laughed. It was such a sincere and infectious laugh that Tony felt warmth fill his chest. "Imagine that! You brought an ancient Kiev-Pechersk Monastery map from America. Incredible!"

She looked again carefully. "Perhaps something was written here a long time ago, but the writing has faded away, leaving just a faint trace. Can you see? There was definitely writing."

"You think so?" Tony peered closely at the faint marks, then at Vera. The last passenger was boarding the bus; any second now, the doors would close.

"I've got to go," Vera said, giving Tony one last lingering look. She smiled, waved, and stepped onto the bus just as the doors hissed shut.

Tony stood quietly as the bus pulled away. A strange emptiness settled inside him as he watched it disappear into traffic. He turned his attention back to the map. It was indeed strange—who could have written something there? Perhaps someone had placed a paper on top, and pressed down too hard.

A peculiar thought crossed Tony's mind: maybe fate had meant for him to write Vera's number precisely on this map. For a moment, he felt as though he were repeating an action already performed in another lifetime, in another world entirely.

Chapter 20

Tony dreamed of Vera. They were strolling slowly through the park as the gentle rays of sunset bathed the domes of Kiev's churches in a golden glow. The dream felt so vivid and real that when Tony opened his eyes, he couldn't immediately understand if he was still in the park or back in his hotel room. The boundary between dream and reality blurred, leaving him disoriented.

He sat up on the bed and held his head between his hands, blinking in confusion. Bright sunlight streamed through the blinds, forming thin stripes across the room. It must already be late morning.

The persistent ringing of the telephone was likely what had awakened him, abruptly tearing him away from the warmth of Vera's embrace and the peaceful beauty of the park. Tony glanced irritably at the intrusive phone and finally picked it up, his movements stiff with annoyance.

At first, Tony didn't grasp why the travel agency representative was calling him, but then remembered that the man had promised to set up a meeting with local businessmen.

"Yes, thank you," he said briefly. "I'll be down in the hotel lobby in a few minutes."

Tony took a quick shower. Within ten minutes, he was downstairs. Though he'd rushed to get ready, he now deliberately moved slowly, appearing as though he'd taken his time to fold a newspaper, rise leisurely from the sofa, and walk casually downstairs. Tony was impeccably dressed and clean-shaven, without the slightest indication that he'd just hurried. Years of experience had taught him to mask any nervousness or hurry, never allowing others to see that their time or opinions mattered more to him than his own.

The travel agency representative waited in the lobby along with two men Tony had never seen before. Tony discreetly glanced at their clothing, immediately noting their expensive suits and meticulous appearance. He hadn't expected Ukrainian businessmen to dress so elegantly; they differed greatly from the modest image he'd previously held in his mind.

One of the men had distinct Asian features—muscular, with broad shoulders and an imposing presence. The other was tall and handsome, with classic Slavic features, and wore an affable smile.

The Slavic-looking man stepped forward and introduced himself as Vladimir, then motioned toward his associate. "And this is my business partner, Rustam," he said, extending his hand to shake Tony's.

"Our young friend here," Vladimir nodded toward the representative, "spoke very highly of you as a businessman interested in investing in Ukraine." Vladimir spoke in a polite, quiet voice. His English was decent, though heavily accented. There was something about his calm demeanor and easy manner that inspired trust.

Tony smiled warmly in return. "Yes, I have a few ideas regarding Ukraine."

Vladimir nodded approvingly. "We would be delighted if your ideas matched our interests. But perhaps we could discuss this somewhere more comfortable?" Vladimir gestured courteously toward the hotel exit.

Outside, a sleek silver Mercedes awaited them. Vladimir guided Tony toward the car, opening the back door and sliding smoothly onto the leather seat next to him. Rustam settled himself in the front passenger seat, beside the driver.

The travel agency representative lingered uncertainly near the car. Vladimir lowered his window slightly and fixed the man with a polite yet chilly gaze.

"You're not thinking of joining us, are you? There's no need. We'll handle everything ourselves. You must have a lot of work to do."

The Mercedes slowly pulled away from the curb. Tony looked back through the window, noticing the representative forcing a polite smile as he waved goodbye, clearly unsettled by the sudden dismissal.

Tony turned to Vladimir, puzzled. "Isn't he coming along?"

Vladimir gave a casual shrug, as if nothing unusual had occurred. "Unfortunately, our young friend is very busy. He's expecting a tour group from London in a few hours, you know how these things are. Tell me, Tony, is this your first visit to Ukraine?"

"Yes," Tony answered briefly.

Vladimir smiled knowingly, his eyes sharp and calculating. "It takes courage to come to an unfamiliar country without friends or family nearby. But you must be careful here; Ukraine can be unpredictable." Vladimir paused slightly, then added, his voice softening, yet carrying an unmistakable edge, "As long as you're with us, you have nothing to worry about."

Tony nodded silently. Despite Vladimir's friendly tone, he sensed an undercurrent of threat beneath the pleasant words. Tony glanced quickly at his Rolex. It read exactly 12:15 p.m.

***

1:10 p.m.

An elegant restaurant in the heart of Kiev. Sunlight filtered softly through wide windows draped with delicate curtains, gently illuminating polished tables adorned with crisp linen and gleaming silverware. Quiet jazz played in the background, mingling with the low murmur of diners' conversations and the discreet clinking of glasses.

Tony sat at a secluded table together with his two new acquaintances, Vladimir and Rustam, who chatted comfortably, their posture relaxed and assured. Tony, however, felt slightly uneasy; his gaze roamed restlessly around the refined décor, the crystal chandeliers casting subtle reflections that danced on the walls.

At that moment, the men rose smoothly from their seats. Tony, following their example, also stood up. Approaching the table was a striking woman with bright blonde hair cascading gently over her shoulders. Her confident walk and long, graceful legs instantly captured attention, turning a few heads around the room.

"Tony, please allow me to introduce you to Oksana," Vladimir said warmly, his smile broadening as he indicated the beautiful newcomer with a gracious gesture. "Unfortunately, my English isn't as perfect as that of our company's lovely manager. Oksana spent some time training in Great Britain, and we're fortunate she's agreed to join us today."

Oksana extended her delicate hand, smiling effortlessly. Her eyes, deep blue and radiant with quiet confidence, met Tony's gaze directly. He felt pleasantly surprised, both by her striking appearance and natural grace. He briefly took her hand, noticing how soft and warm it felt in his own.

"It's nice to meet you, Tony," she said gently, taking the seat beside him with fluid elegance. Her English indeed carried the smooth, sophisticated accent of someone comfortable abroad.

Tony smiled appreciatively, his initial tension dissipating slightly. "Your English is remarkable," he complimented sincerely.

Oksana tilted her head, the corners of her lips curving slightly upward, her voice light and engaging. "We do business with many Western companies," she explained casually, sensing Tony's curiosity. "Our international partners often come to Kiev, giving me plenty of practice with the language."

As she spoke, Tony found himself relaxing more fully. There was something reassuring and magnetic about her presence as if Oksana effortlessly bridged the distance between the familiar and the unknown. Glancing briefly at Vladimir and Rustam, who had resumed their comfortable positions at the table, Tony began to feel cautiously optimistic about this unexpected encounter.

***

1:15 p.m.

Vera stepped into the church's archive, a cool, shadowy place hidden in an old semi-basement building. It was a place she had always loved—full of secrets, ancient manuscripts, and forgotten history. Tall wooden shelves, polished by time, stood so densely packed that they formed a labyrinth, dimly lit by weak sunlight filtering through the narrow windows near the high ceiling. The air was heavy with the scent of old paper, leather bindings, and the faint fragrance of wax.

At the faint creak of the door behind her, Vera turned quickly. A thin, aged monk stepped from between the towering bookcases, his worn cassock rustling softly. The old man's pale eyes lit up in genuine pleasure as he recognized her, and a warm smile spread across his wrinkled face.

"Vera, my dear, what brings you here today?"

Father Ilarion was the soul of this place; no one remembered the monastery without him. It was impossible to guess his age, for he seemed timeless.

"How are you feeling today, Father Ilarion?" Vera asked gently, approaching.

The monk gave a weak wave of his hand. "Oh, nothing new, my child. My heart misbehaves sometimes, but what else is there to expect at my age? God keeps me around for some reason."

Vera smiled warmly, then paused, slightly hesitant. "Father, I need your help today. One of my tourists asked me something, and I had no idea how to answer."

The monk raised his eyebrows in amused disbelief. "You? Unable to answer a question about our monastery? That's impossible, Vera! You know these grounds better than most monks who live here."

Vera felt her cheeks growing hot, and she looked down at her shoes. "Father, now you're contradicting yourself. Weren't you the one who always said it's impossible to know everything?"

Father Ilarion nodded knowingly, gently placing his hand on her shoulder. "You're right, my child. I say that to remind my students never to grow complacent. But I am truly pleased you are still seeking new answers. So tell me, what is troubling you today?"

Vera hesitated briefly. "I need information about Saint Antony's will. And, if possible, I'd like to know whether anyone has ever attempted to open his tomb."

The smile vanished immediately from Father Ilarion's face, replaced by a guarded expression. "Why would you need to know something like that?" His voice sounded quieter now, cautious.

Vera shrugged gently, trying to appear casual. "It's just curiosity, Father. Nothing more. Can you help me?"

The monk studied her silently for a long moment as though debating with himself. Then, without another word, he turned, beckoning her deeper into the maze-like stacks of books. Vera followed carefully, stepping softly, her heart beating quicker as they moved into the shadowy depths of the archive.

They stopped before a dark, forgotten corner. Father Ilarion paused before an ancient wooden bookcase, its doors framed in ornate carvings, the glass dusty from years of neglect. The monk carefully opened the case and gently withdrew a faded manuscript, its leather cover cracked with age.

"This is what you seek," he said gravely, handing the manuscript. Then he looked directly into Vera's eyes, his voice barely above a whisper: "But remember —knowledge is like fire. Handle it carelessly, and you may be burned."

With those final words, the old monk turned and silently walked away, leaving Vera alone with the manuscript.

***

4:00 p.m.

The meeting at the restaurant was drawing to a close, and Tony felt genuinely pleased. Everything had gone even better than he'd hoped. Right from the start, he'd sensed that the people across from him were experienced and highly driven businessmen.

"You know," Tony said, leaning forward slightly, "I can only dream of profits like the ones you're making from your vodka business. I'd love to visit your factory, take a look for myself, and learn more about how you operate."

Vladimir nodded, smiling broadly. "We'll arrange that. Let's see… Tomorrow's a bit busy for me, but how about the morning after?"

"That sounds great," Tony replied with enthusiasm. "Works perfectly for me."

"Excellent." Vladimir looked satisfied. "And so you're not bored sitting around your hotel, perhaps Oksana here can show you around Kiev." He glanced warmly at the young woman. "Is that okay with you, Oksana?"

Oksana laughed lightly, her smile genuine and welcoming. "Of course. I'd be happy to."

"Then it's all settled," Vladimir said firmly, shaking Tony's hand. "Rustam will drive you back to your hotel now. Oksana will get in touch with you later to set everything up."

After Tony had left with Rustam, Vladimir exhaled deeply and gestured for Oksana to come closer. She obediently took a seat beside him.

"I think you understand me just fine, Oksana," Vladimir said coldly, his voice dripping with disdain. "You heard him yourself. The guy's loaded, and he's practically begging to spend his cash. So get to work."

He leaned closer, his expression turning harsh and mocking. "You know exactly how these foreigners act around our local girls—they're all the same. Smile, flirt, spread your legs if you have to, I don't care. Just make damn sure he's eating from your hand by tomorrow."

***

4:10 p.m.

Vera rose abruptly from the table. Holding the ancient manuscripts tightly against herself as if they could shield her from unseen danger, she quickly moved toward the archive's exit.

"Father Hilarion!" she called, louder than she'd intended. Her voice echoed sharply through the empty room, betraying her distress.

The elderly archivist glanced up, his eyes clouded by age yet still sharp with curiosity.

"Father Hilarion," Vera said breathlessly, approaching the frail old monk, "many people have tried to uncover the remains of Saint Antony over the last thousand years, but no one succeeded. The ancient chronicles clearly state that everyone who attempted it was 'punished by flames set free,' and spent the remainder of their lives in repentance."

She nervously brushed her tangled hair from her face, her gaze fixed pleadingly on the monk. "Tell me, why was the original Life of Saint Antony destroyed? I've found references and fragments but no original manuscript. Who destroyed it, Father? And why?"

The old monk's serene expression slowly faded, replaced by cautious suspicion. He hesitated, then softly shook his head. "You're mistaken, Vera. The monastic chronicles do contain 'The Life and Mission of Saint Antony.'"

Vera glanced over her shoulder involuntarily, suddenly uneasy, feeling as if unseen eyes were watching them. The archive's silence seemed heavier now.

"What we have," she said softly but insistently, "is nothing more than a brief legend, a beautiful fable. But the actual historical biography, the complete life of Antony, isn't here."

Father Hilarion remained silent, his eyes flickering with uncertainty.

"Please," Vera pressed anxiously, stepping closer, "why was Feodosiy, Antony's disciple, canonized first in 1108, while Saint Antony, the very founder of the monastery, was placed behind him? And why," her voice trembled, "is Antony's tomb sealed so strictly? Even after a thousand years, no one is allowed to see his relics. Why?"

Father Hilarion's eyes filled with sadness. He lowered his gaze, avoiding Vera's piercing stare.

"You know the answer, Father Hilarion. You must know! Tell me—what is hidden in his tomb?"

The old monk sighed deeply, gathering himself, and raised his tired eyes to hers. "The answer lies within your question. If you can ask the right questions, then perhaps you're ready to learn the truth. But remember: knowledge can be dangerous."

Father Hilarion paused, his voice growing weaker. "Vera, I'm very tired. Please come back tomorrow. We'll speak then."

Vera searched his aged, weary face desperately, longing to argue, but finally gave in. "Will you promise to tell me everything tomorrow?"

"I promise," the monk said softly, gently guiding her toward the exit.

After closing the door behind her, Father Hilarion slowly returned to the manuscripts Vera had studied. His fingers trembled slightly as he touched the worn pages, deep in thought. Suddenly, he flinched, glancing nervously around the archive. For a brief, unsettling moment, he had the distinct feeling that someone else was there, silently watching him from the shadows.

Chapter 21

After the meeting with Vladimir and Rustam, Tony returned to his hotel room. He took a long, hot shower, hoping the water would wash away the tension still lingering from his meeting. He carefully selected a fresh shirt from the closet and stood for a moment, adjusting his cuffs. But his mind kept wandering.

Tony glanced at his watch, listened to the distant murmur of evening traffic outside the hotel window, and sat on the edge of the bed. The folded monastery map lay next to him, worn from his fingers, constantly turning it over and over again. He picked it up once more.

Why was he so hesitant? Normally, Tony knew exactly what he wanted and how to get it. At home, he rarely struggled with indecision; in business, he always acted decisively, moving from one strategic choice to another. But here, in this unfamiliar city, he felt strangely vulnerable. He closed his eyes and saw Vera clearly—the soft, quiet depth of her gaze, her graceful, subtle gestures as she spoke about the monastery, the gentle movement of her hands when she fixed her hair. She was unlike any woman he had met before.

Doubt crept into his mind, whispering uncertainty. What if Vera had forgotten him already? What if, to her, he was merely another foreign tourist, one of dozens who wandered through the monastery's sacred grounds every day? He imagined her confusion or polite indifference when she heard his voice on the phone, and the thought made him tense.

But the pull to see her again, to talk to her even once more, was stronger than any worry. Tony drew a deep breath, brushed away a bead of nervous sweat from his forehead, and picked up the phone. He dialed slowly, each number pressed carefully, as though that alone might influence her answer.

The dial tone rang in his ear, each ring stretching out and deepening his anxiety. He stood up from the bed and began pacing quietly, feeling his heart quicken in anticipation, the sounds of Kiev fading into the background as he waited for her voice.

***

Tony waited for Vera near the gates of the Kiev-Pechersk Monastery. She had refused to come to his hotel, and he knew nowhere else to suggest. So now Tony wandered quietly back and forth along the wide boulevard, glancing at his watch more often than he cared to admit. He had arrived far too early, his heart restless with anticipation.

As he paced, Tony replayed their earlier phone conversation in his mind. He still couldn't believe Vera had recognized his voice immediately.

"Tony? Hello. I've been thinking about you today," she had said, her voice warm and surprisingly intimate.

"You really were thinking about me?" he'd asked, astonished and pleased.

"Of course. By the way, I never lie." She had laughed gently, almost teasing him. "Remember when you asked about Saint Anthony? I went to the archives today, and—"

"Did you find out something new?" Tony interrupted, his pulse quickening. "Vera, can we meet tonight? You could tell me more about Saint Anthony, show me Kiev—and I promise you the most wonderful dinner you've ever had. Where should we meet? I'm sorry, but I only know the hotel and the monastery..."

Now, the golden sunset poured its last rays over the ancient domes of the churches, turning them a rich honey color before gently sinking into the distant waters of the Dnieper. Soft twilight began to settle over Kiev, cloaking the city in violet shadows.

Tony turned sharply as a taxi pulled up nearby. A young woman stepped gracefully from the car. His heart skipped a beat. It was Vera, yet not quite the same woman he'd met yesterday. This Vera wore a light blouse, and her skirt ended well above her knees, accentuating slender legs he'd barely glimpsed before. Tony felt a slight flush rise to his cheeks as he struggled for words.

"Hello, Tony!" she greeted him brightly.

For a moment, Tony hesitated, completely taken aback. "Oh... hi!" he stammered awkwardly, smiling shyly. "For a second, I was afraid you might not come."

Vera laughed, her eyes shining playfully. "Well, here I am." Without hesitation, she stepped forward and gently took his hand, pulling him toward the walkway.

Tony tried to pinpoint exactly what was different about her. She was the same woman, with the same dark, expressive eyes and warm, genuine smile. Yet now, away from the monastery's strict walls, Vera moved freely and spoke openly as though a layer of invisible tension had dissolved around her.

As they walked, Tony found himself completely at ease in her company, their conversation flowing naturally. For the first time in a very long while, he felt truly comfortable, as if they had known each other forever. It took him several moments to understand why. It was because of the way she now looked at him—not as a mere visitor, but as someone genuinely interesting to her, someone worth knowing more deeply.

He felt a gentle warmth spread through his chest—a sensation different from ordinary desire. It rose softly, organically, from somewhere deeper, filling him with an unfamiliar tenderness.

He couldn't recall ever feeling this way before, and the realization both thrilled and unsettled him.

Without noticing, they wandered through city parks and quiet, tree-lined alleys until darkness enveloped Kiev. Eventually, they stopped by the Mariinsky Palace, standing quietly side by side, looking out at the shimmering lights reflected across the dark expanse of the Dnieper.

"I never imagined Ukraine could be so beautiful," Tony whispered thoughtfully, breaking the comfortable silence. "Now I see why people fought so hard for this land. Every piece of earth here has been touched by blood and passion..."

Vera turned to him, her eyes searching his face. "Have you ever loved deeply, Tony?"

"Loved deeply?" He paused, thoughtfully considering her question. "I don't know... I suppose not. I've never found a woman I could see myself spending my life with."

She tilted her head slightly, her eyes softening. "You say that with such sadness. Why?"

Tony smiled ruefully. "Because, until I came here, my life was just drifting along, aimless. I felt comfortable—like being in a hammock between two palm trees. I never stopped to think about who I really was or why I was here."

He reached out instinctively and placed a gentle hand on Vera's shoulder, but she carefully, softly removed it.

Changing the subject, Tony asked gently, "So tell me—why did you choose history? There are so many other fields of study."

She shrugged lightly, gazing out over the city. "Maybe because I've always felt safer among books than among people. Books never betray you, they never hurt you."

He looked at her closely. "Have you been hurt often?"

"Sometimes." Her voice softened, becoming nearly a whisper.

"What about men? A woman as beautiful as you must have plenty of admirers."

Vera laughed softly, shaking her head. "Plenty or few, it doesn't matter. It's not their feelings for me that count, but mine for them. Most men only see my outward appearance and don't care to look beyond it."

"But not all men are—" Tony began.

She interrupted gently, smiling. "Men are different, yet somehow always the same."

Tony felt an odd pang of sympathy—for himself, for Vera, for everyone. "The same could be said of women. People are like books on a shelf. You might ignore some entirely, while others you come back to again and again, finding something new and fascinating each time."

She looked at him with an amused twinkle in her eye. "And which book are you reading right now, Tony—from America?"

He hesitated, suddenly shy. "Right now? None, really…"

Vera fixed him with an intense, penetrating gaze. Then, very quietly, she smiled and said, "You're lying."

***

Tony and Vera couldn't have known that at the very same moment, a procession of monks, their faces hidden beneath black hoods, moved silently through the monastery grounds. Their steps were slow and deliberate, the quiet rustling of their robes blending with the distant, mournful tolling of church bells.

They walked solemnly toward the Near Caves, their features expressionless in the flickering candlelight, their shadows stretching across the ancient stone walls. Two monks carried between them a heavy burden carefully wrapped in black cloth.

At the mouth of the caves, the group stopped abruptly, their breath forming faint clouds in the chill night air. An older monk stepped forward, his face concealed by the deep shadows of his hood.

"It is time," he spoke softly, yet his voice resonated clearly through the darkness.

A young novice hesitated, nervously glancing around as if sensing some unseen presence watching from the shadows.

"But Father," he whispered anxiously, unable to hide the fear in his voice, "is this right?"

"Silence," commanded the older monk sharply, though a weary note lingered in his tone.

As if responding to his words, a sudden gust of wind swept through the trees, extinguishing half of their candles at once. The monks froze, startled. The covered body appeared to shudder slightly—or perhaps it was just an illusion cast by the flickering shadows. From deep within the cave's dark entrance came a distant whisper, indistinct but unmistakably human.

The older monk raised a trembling hand. "We must hurry."

***

Vera lived in the center of Kiev, about ten minutes from the park. They approached an old building with peculiar architecture and climbed a wide, ornate staircase to the third floor. It was a striking structure, unlike anything Tony had seen around Kiev so far.

As Vera opened the apartment door, the first thing Tony noticed was the sheer number of books lining the shelves and antique maps decorating the walls. The ceilings rose high above him, much taller than those in the apartments he knew back in Chicago, giving the room an open, airy feeling despite the clutter.

"You live here alone?" Tony asked, glancing around curiously.

"With my parents," Vera replied lightly, slipping off her shoes. "But during warmer months, they prefer to stay in our country house."

She paused and looked at Tony, a warm, inviting smile touching her lips. "Would you like anything? Tea? Something to eat?"

"No, thank you," Tony answered, moving towards a small table displaying family photographs. He picked one up, examining it closely. "You were so funny when you were little."

Vera emerged from the kitchen carrying a tray with a teapot and a box of chocolates, her expression a playful mixture of embarrassment and amusement.

"I don't see anything funny about it," she protested gently, setting the tray carefully on the coffee table. "I was just a child like any other."

Tony's gaze softened as he studied the photo, then glanced back at her with a teasing grin. "Even as a child, you already had the look of a fatal woman."

Vera laughed softly, shaking her head. She caught her reflection in the mirror and examined herself with mock seriousness.

"Oh, please! I don't see anything 'fatal' here," she said with playful skepticism.

Tony stepped closer, placing a gentle hand on her shoulder and softly turning her towards him.

"Vera, you're not looking in the right place."

Her eyes widened slightly, curious and questioning. "What do you mean?"

"To see the true reflection of a woman, you need to look into the eyes of the man who admires her."

Her lips, so close to his, were calling him to heaven.

Chapter 22

Tony was amazed. Vera seemed reluctant, mysterious, and unattainable—like a distant star from another galaxy whose light he could see but never touch. Throughout their conversation, she kept an invisible distance, a subtle yet firm line Tony dared not cross. Her voice was gentle, her laughter light, but there was always something in her eyes—a quiet caution—that reminded him she wasn't within easy reach.

When Vera softly but clearly hinted that their evening had come to an end, Tony wasn't surprised. He understood. This was Vera: she wasn't someone who could be hurried, let alone pressured. Without awkwardness or disappointment, they stepped outside together, into the cool night air that gently whispered through the empty streets. Side by side, their steps fell in a comforting rhythm as they walked towards Tony's hotel.

The night air carried faint scents of lilac from distant gardens, mingling with Vera's own subtle perfume—a blend so delicate, it reminded Tony of something precious and rare. He glanced sideways at her profile, half-lit by streetlamps: the curve of her cheek, the slight turn of her lips, the way she tucked a loose strand of hair behind her ear. Every gesture was careful, precise, perfectly measured. He suddenly realized how comfortable he felt beside her, despite her gentle but unwavering boundaries.

Vera was nothing like Sofia, Tony thought. Sofia was bold, fierce, her passion always burning close to the surface. He recalled her eyes—fearless, challenging, always ready for confrontation. She had known exactly what she wanted, and how to take it. Yet, Tony realized, something had always felt rough and unfinished about their relationship—something missing. With Vera, everything felt softer, more nuanced. Even in her rejection, there was a tenderness that intrigued him deeply.

They paused briefly at the entrance of the hotel. Tony looked at Vera, feeling an unexpected warmth rise within him.

"You know, Vera," Tony said sincerely, meeting her calm, questioning gaze, "you really are the most beautiful woman in the world. No, honestly. I mean it—the most beautiful."

Vera laughed softly, shaking her head, her eyes glinting with gentle amusement.

"Oh, Tony," she said, a playful seriousness coloring her voice, "you Americans really do love exaggerating."

Her laughter was warm, effortless, sincere—yet Tony noticed how quickly she shifted the conversation, smoothly guiding them back to safer territory, away from compliments she wasn't ready to accept. Still, the feeling of her hand briefly touching his arm as she turned to leave sent a wave of warmth through him, confirming what he already knew: Vera was special, unlike anyone he had ever met. And even as he watched her walk away, gracefully disappearing into the quiet night, Tony felt not rejection but a hopeful kind of comfort.

***

Tony returned to his room and immediately headed for the bathroom. Ever since childhood, he'd found a bath to be a small luxury—a place of peace where he could briefly escape from reality. This bathtub was too cramped for his tall frame, but he didn't care. After the tense, bewildering day he'd just had, this small comfort was exactly what he needed.

He turned on the water, adjusting it to a perfect, steamy heat. Slowly lowering himself into the bathtub, he sighed in relief as the warmth immediately began to melt away the day's stress. The room filled with mist, carrying the faint scent of hotel soap, reminding him briefly of Vera's subtle fragrance—a gentle aroma, elusive but unforgettable.

As Tony lay back, sinking deeper into the hot, bubbly water, he let his eyes drift shut. His muscles began to unclench, tension dissolving from his shoulders, his back, his legs. The colorful bubbles floated lazily on the water's surface, catching reflections of the bathroom's dim lighting, shimmering softly like tiny rainbows.

His thoughts wandered leisurely, drifting into pleasant daydreams. How wonderful it would be, he thought, to inherit a million dollars. Imagine: no more waking up early for work, no endless meetings, no stressful negotiations.

The soothing warmth spread through his body, carrying him deeper into his fantasy. The room seemed to fade away slowly, replaced by images of beautiful beaches, turquoise waves gently lapping the shore, the warmth of Vera's touch, and the sweetness of her quiet laughter. Tony's breathing slowed, becoming soft and regular.

Just feet away, in the room outside, the telephone rang insistently, its sharp sound slicing through the quiet. It rang again and again, the urgency of each ring growing more intense. But Tony heard nothing, far away in a world of dreams. His head tilted back against the porcelain edge of the bathtub, his breathing deep and even.

He was already fast asleep.

***

The unfamiliar monk stood silently by the table, watching Vera carefully as she entered the archives. She paused, startled.

She thought she knew every face here, every monk who worked in these quiet rooms filled with ancient manuscripts. Yet this tall, imposing figure, about forty years old, was completely unknown to her.

"What do you want?" the monk asked, his voice even and cold.

Vera glanced around anxiously, searching for the kind, familiar face of Father Hilarion. But the elderly monk was nowhere to be seen. Instead, the stranger stood motionless at the very table where Father Hilarion usually sat, calmly returning Vera's bewildered gaze.

"I wanted to speak with Father Hilarion," Vera said softly.

The monk slowly stood up, approaching her. "Father Hilarion is dead."

Vera felt as if something heavy had suddenly fallen inside her chest. She instinctively took a step backward. This was the last thing she'd expected to hear.

"That can't be true. When? What happened?" Her voice trembled.

"Yesterday," the monk replied calmly. "He had a weak heart."

His indifferent, almost mechanical tone unnerved Vera deeply. Only those who had become too accustomed to death spoke of it so coldly.

"But that can't be right," she whispered, mostly to herself. "I saw him yesterday…"

"We know," the monk said simply, looking her straight in the eye.

Something about the way he spoke, something hidden in his words, sent a wave of fear through Vera. Her heart beat faster.

"When is the funeral?" she asked quietly.

"He has already been buried."

"What?" Vera moved toward the door, her voice edged with disbelief. The monk made no move to stop her, but spoke again, his tone unchanged.

"He was buried last night."

"Why at night?" Vera asked, turning around sharply.

The stranger raised an eyebrow slightly, as though surprised by her question. "You've worked at Kiev-Pechersk Monastery long enough to know that the authorities don't allow burials here anymore. But monks who've earned special respect still wish to rest in this sacred place. We bury them quietly, secretly, under cover of darkness, so that the government won't interfere."

Vera lowered her eyes, saddened. "Then I won't even be able to lay flowers on his grave…"

"If you wish, you can place them near the entrance to the Near Caves."

Vera opened the door slightly, hesitating before leaving. "He wanted to tell me something important yesterday."

"Vera," the monk said suddenly. "That is your name, isn't it?"

Surprised, she turned to face him again. "Yes. Do we know each other?"

He paused, watching her intently. Then he said, very slowly, "If Father Hilarion were still alive, perhaps he'd tell you that God often calls to Himself first those who ask too many questions."

***

The cold woke Tony. He lay motionless in the bath, his skin pale from the chilly water. Shivering slightly, he got up slowly, wrapped himself in a robe, and walked out into the room. He glanced at the clock and couldn't believe his eyes—he'd slept in the bath for nearly half the day.

Oddly enough, he felt strangely refreshed and even energetic. With a carefree ease he hadn't felt in days, Tony sat down beside the old box of his grandfather's belongings that his mother had given him. Absently, he flipped open the lid and began sorting through the contents: yellowed papers, faded photographs of people he didn't recognize, distant streets, and unfamiliar buildings.

He could probably find some of these places if he tried, but right now he had no real desire to chase ghosts. Tony paused, his eyes resting on a black-and-white photo of his grandfather. Something about the image troubled him, a quiet, nagging sensation. That particular look, the tilt of his head, the intensity in his grandfather's gaze—he had seen it before.

"But where?" he whispered, feeling uneasy.

Then it hit him. The realization struck Tony like lightning, making his pulse race and filling his chest with anxious excitement. The Kiev-Pechersk Monastery. The Near Caves. The image of Saint Antony. The likeness was unmistakable.

Cold sweat broke out across his forehead. The resemblance was uncanny; it was as if his grandfather and Saint Antony were staring at him with identical eyes across the centuries.

Tony jumped up, adrenaline surging through him, and grabbed the phone, dialing frantically.

"Vera! Vera, listen carefully, this is incredibly important. I've finally understood everything my grandfather was trying to tell me. Remember when I told you about his will—that if I fulfilled all the conditions, I'd get something more valuable than just three million dollars here in Ukraine? Something he couldn't take with him to America? It didn't make any sense to me until now. But I see it clearly now!"

Tony spoke rapidly, his voice full of excitement, almost manic. He didn't even notice the alarm rising in Vera's voice.

"Tony, slow down. What are you saying? What's going on?"

"Listen carefully! I had to come here. This was all destined. I'm named after Saint Antony. Remember the handful of soil? It's all connected. My grandfather had something incredibly valuable, jewels perhaps, and needed a safe place—somewhere nobody would dare disturb, not during wars, not during revolutions, never. Think about it: Saint Antony's tomb has remained untouched for almost a thousand years. It's the perfect hiding place!"

"Tony, you're not making sense. Please calm down," Vera pleaded, her voice trembling with fear. "You're scaring me."

But Tony didn't hear her. He couldn't stop himself.

"Vera, remember how strange I felt when we saw the icon of Saint Antony? I told you then, the expression seemed familiar. And now I know why: my grandfather's photograph—it's the same look, the exact same expression as Saint Antony's icon. It's no coincidence. Don't you see? The photograph is the key!"

"Tony, listen to yourself! You're delusional," Vera protested desperately. Panic tightened around her heart. She could feel the danger lurking in his words, something frighteningly unstoppable.

But Tony would not be swayed. He spoke with absolute certainty.

"No, Vera, no more arguments. I'm coming over right now. You have to help me. Together we'll open Saint Antony's grave."

Chapter 23

Greed is the true motivator of civilization. It has the power to pull people out of warm beds and thrust them into cold winds. America itself was founded on greed. Everything that people admire about their ancestors is ultimately a product of greed. If not for hypocrisy, monuments dedicated to Her Majesty Greed would stand proudly in every city, town, and village. People often underestimate its strength, yet greed can suppress fear and override instincts. It can empower even the weakest among us.

Tony ran to the Kiev-Pechersk Monastery without bothering to dress properly. He had thrown on the first shirt he found, not caring whether it was wrinkled or neat. The idea that he had finally discovered the hiding place of the jewels drove him almost mad. He had no doubt those jewels would make him unimaginably rich, and the glorious vision of endless wealth consumed his mind.

He didn't notice Vera's distress. She stood quietly, trying to understand what had happened to him in such a short time. It felt as though a stranger stood before her, someone entirely different from the Tony she thought she knew.

"Tony, I don't even know how to stop you," Vera said, shaking her head sadly. "It's insane. Forget this crazy idea. Besides, I don't even know how you'd do it. No one would ever give you permission to open the grave of a saint."

"You see!" Tony interrupted greedily. "Even you admit the main obstacle is getting permission—not whether we should open it at all."

"Don't put words in my mouth!" Vera snapped angrily. She felt utterly exhausted, as though a heavy weight had dropped onto her shoulders. "I'm completely against opening the grave. I have a very bad feeling about it."

"Who cares about your feelings?" Tony shouted, losing patience. "Someone will open it sooner or later. Why should somebody else find those jewels and not us? Vera, just imagine—we'd be rich! We could do anything we want without ever worrying about money again. Rich!"

Vera stared into Tony's eyes, her voice trembling with disappointment. "Aren't you already rich enough? Isn't that enough for you?"

"There's no such thing as enough money! If fate gives us an opportunity like this, we must take it—otherwise, I'd lose all respect for myself."

Vera shook her head slowly. "Right now, you sound exactly like every other American I've ever met. You dismiss other nations' traditions and rituals as worthless. Money is your only god."

Tony's face twisted with anger. "And what do you Ukrainians have? Have you ever asked yourself why Ukraine is still so far behind the rest of the world? It's because you're all afraid to look reality in the eye. The truth scares you; your own history scares you. Even events that happened a thousand years ago still hold you back with superstition. Your traditions keep you poor, always begging for help from more developed countries."

Vera turned away abruptly.

Tony paused, realizing he'd crossed a line. "I'm sorry," he said quietly. "I didn't mean to upset you."

They walked silently through the monastery grounds.

"Tony, I honestly don't know how to change your mind," Vera finally said, breaking the painful silence. "You need to talk to my brother. Remember the photos of him at my place? I'm sure he can help." Her voice was uncertain and hollow.

Tony nodded eagerly. "Set up a meeting with him—the sooner, the better. He's a businessman; we'll find a way to talk."

They stopped near the entrance to the Near Caves. Vera knelt slowly and placed a lilac branch gently on the ground. Tears welled in her eyes.

"Why is money the only thing you care about? Why?" Vera suddenly broke down, covering her face with her hands as she sobbed.

"Vera…" Tony hesitated, unsure what to do. He reached out to comfort her, but she stepped away from him.

"Vera, please," Tony said helplessly. "Listen to me..."

Chapter 24

Vera's brother was shorter than she was. Because of this, he wore shoes with thick platform soles to appear taller and more confident. For the same reason, he grew a neatly trimmed beard and wore gold-rimmed glasses, even though his eyesight was perfectly fine.

His glasses lay on the table as he stood brushing his teeth while Vera spoke to him about Tony.

"I don't need your American," Vasily grumbled through a mouthful of toothpaste. "Do you know how many like him I see every day? Each one claims to have millions." He paused, turned aside, and blew his nose loudly. "Funny thing is, none of them ever actually lose their money. They have everything they could ever want—connections all over the world. But when it comes to real work, to real investment, where are they? Not one cent ever comes out of their pockets. They talk endlessly about grand projects, but lift a finger? Never."

"Tony isn't like that," Vera insisted gently.

"They're all the same," her brother responded skeptically. "Especially Americans." He rinsed his toothbrush, examining the bristles carefully. "Anyway, what kind of business does he have in the States? Who is he exactly?"

Vera settled onto a small stool in the living room, watching her brother's reflection in the bathroom mirror. "He's an electrical engineer, working in the aircraft industry. Most of his money came from an inheritance. Now he wants to start his own business."

Vasily made a skeptical sound. "Sounds like he has no idea what it means to run your own business. In America, people study one narrow specialty, and then think they can do anything..." His last words drowned in the sound of running water from the faucet. Then he continued clearly, "He might know aircraft and electronics, but as far as business here goes, he'll end up either losing all his money or backing out completely."

Vera nodded patiently. "That's exactly why I want you to meet him and talk things over."

The water roared again, and Vasily blew his nose once more— so loudly this time that Vera flinched, feeling sudden worry for her brother's health.

"Sister," he sighed, "it's just a waste of time. I don't need him or his inheritance. I'll raise the money myself. If I can't find it, I'll earn it." He stepped out of the bathroom doorway, still holding his damp towel. His eyes flashed with sudden passion. "You'll see, Vera. I'm going to invest every penny in the restoration of the Kiev-Pechersk Monastery. I'll build a new Kiev. Our great-grandfather built a church in Chernigov, and I'll build a new capital—the heart of a revived Ukraine. It'll mark the beginning of our true renaissance! Then Ukraine will finally become an independent nation!" Vasily waved his toothbrush in the air dramatically. "Future generations will write our names in golden letters!"

Vera glanced sadly at the pile of books scattered carelessly in the middle of the room. "Why are all the men in my life a little strange? Not just a little, either—very strange. One wants to dig up Saint Antony's grave chasing some mythical jewels, another dreams obsessively about his glorious ancestors…"

Vasily emerged fully from the bathroom, vigorously drying his hair. "Why so mean to me, sister?" He grinned softly, shaking his head. "Fine. Bring your American. I'll talk to him."

Chapter 25

Oksana dialed Tony's number again from Vladimir's office—for what felt like the hundredth time—but he still didn't answer. Frustrated, she tossed the phone aside.

"Damn American. Where the hell is he?" she muttered just as the phone rang again. This time, it was Vladimir's secretary.

"Oksana? The boss wants to see you."

Oksana glanced quickly at her reflection in the small mirror she kept in her purse. She looked fine. Good enough for Vladimir, at least.

Vladimir sat comfortably in his chair, legs propped casually on a richly decorated antique table. His office was filled with similar rarities, making it resemble a private museum rather than a workspace.

"So, where's our American?" Vladimir drawled lazily as Oksana entered.

"I can't reach him."

"What do you mean you can't?" Vladimir gave her a contemptuous smile. "Then go find him. Check the hotel bar. He doesn't have anyone here except a bunch of dead ancestors."

"I already went there." Oksana lowered her voice guiltily. "He wasn't there."

Vladimir yawned, clicking absently on the laptop balanced on his lap. When he had nothing better to do, he usually played solitaire.

"Then you didn't look hard enough. If he slips away, it'll be your head."

"Please don't be angry." Oksana smiled weakly, hoping to ease his mood.

Rustam burst into the office without knocking. "Here," he said, handing Vladimir a phone. "It's the American."

Vladimir raised an eyebrow. "Really? What did he say?"

"I don't know!" Rustam waved dismissively as he turned back to the door. "He's speaking his language, not ours. You talk to him yourself."

As the door closed behind Rustam, Vladimir rose smoothly from his seat and spoke into the phone in heavily accented English. "Tony! How's your vacation going?"

"Excellent!" Tony sounded cheerful. "Kiev's an amazing city. Listen, Vladimir, sorry, but there's a slight change in plans. Can we move our visit to the factory to the day after tomorrow?"

Vladimir shot a sharp look at Oksana, though his voice remained friendly. "Of course, Tony. Our plans revolve around you. You're our guest; hospitality matters greatly to us. Is everything all right? Need any help?"

"No, everything's perfect! There's just so much to do and so little time. My friends unexpectedly arranged an important meeting tomorrow, and I can't reschedule it. Sorry if it causes any inconvenience."

Vladimir struggled to keep his voice calm. "Don't worry about it. It's fine. So, we'll pick you up at nine the day after tomorrow. Hopefully, nothing else changes in your plans."

"Thanks for understanding, Vladimir. Bye!"

"Goodbye." Vladimir set down the phone, turning a furious glare on Oksana.

"What the hell was that?" he hissed through clenched teeth. "Friends? A business meeting? Who exactly were you supposed to be watching, you stupid bitch?"

Before Oksana could respond, Vladimir slapped her hard across the face. She raised her hands to shield herself, but he grabbed a fistful of her hair, forcing her roughly onto her knees in front of him.

"Vladimir, please…" Oksana whispered, trembling as she fumbled to unfasten his pants. Her slender fingers shook slightly, the delicate ring on her right hand catching the light.

She gripped Vladimir's hips hard, kissing him desperately, feverishly. A shiver of wild pleasure surged through his body, feeding his arrogance and strengthening his sense of power. Vladimir looked down at her with cold contempt, noticing smudges of her lipstick leaving traces on his skin and pants. He roughly tangled his fingers in her hair and pulled her forcefully to her feet, ignoring her sharp gasp of pain. Spinning her around, he shoved her forward, pressing her down onto the antique table until the wood creaked beneath her.

Chapter 26

"Vasily Petrovich, your sister is here with the American," the secretary announced, pausing at the door to await an answer.

Vasily stood up from behind his desk, scratching the back of his head. "Make them something—tea or coffee—and show them in."

Vasily's office reminded Tony of an aquarium. Behind the glass walls, his employees drifted silently back and forth, papers clutched in their hands, lips moving without sound. It was impossible to tell who was actually in the aquarium—whether it was Vasily, observing his employees, or his staff quietly spying on their boss's every move.

Whenever interviewed, Vasily liked to boast that the glass walls had been custom-designed to match his modern tastes, but in reality, they'd simply been the cheapest option available at the time.

Vasily desperately wanted to appear rich and influential. He wanted the world to believe he was someone who could make things happen, a man in control. But despite owning his business, he had neither substantial wealth nor powerful connections, and this always weighed heavily on him.

Born into a humble peasant family, Vasily had risen far above his origins through sheer determination and intelligence, excelling at his studies and building his own company. Yet two things still gnawed relentlessly at his self-esteem.

The first was an unspoken rivalry with his former classmates, many of whom had managed to accumulate greater wealth and social status. Vasily couldn't tolerate the thought of lagging behind—his pride demanded first place and anything less felt like a failure.

But the second was even harder to bear. Vera had been adopted by Vasily's family when she was barely six months old after her noble-born parents tragically died in a car accident. Vasily truly loved his adopted sister, but as they both grew up, it became painfully obvious to him that they were fundamentally different.

Vera carried herself with an innate aristocratic elegance, something deeply embedded in her very blood, passed down through generations. Everyone, including Vasily's own parents, had always admired her gentle refinement and her effortless sophistication. And no matter how successful he became, Vasily knew he would always remain just a peasant beneath the surface. Secretly, bitterly, he envied Vera's noble heritage.

Driven by this hidden insecurity, Vasily obsessively researched historical archives, hoping to uncover a distant noble ancestor who would somehow validate his place in the world. His ambitious project to restore Kiev-Pechersk Monastery was his grandest attempt to fulfill his craving for prestige. Single and without family obligations, he poured all his energy into this goal.

When Tony stepped into Vasily's office, he immediately noticed the collection of monastery maps and intricately carved souvenir statues lining the shelves. They gave the room an exotic, appealing atmosphere.

"Even the richest businessmen in America wouldn't have an office this luxurious," Tony complimented sincerely as he entered.

"Well, that's because in your country, people hurry from work to home," Vasily responded, gesturing casually toward a leather sofa. "Here, it's the opposite—we hurry from home to work. Most of our lives are spent in offices like this."

He sat down opposite Tony, ignoring the disapproving glance Vera cast in his direction. She disliked it when her brother tried to impress guests with exaggerated confidence.

"Did Vera already explain to you what we're doing here?" Vasily asked, his English heavily accented but clear.

Tony nodded. "She did, briefly."

"Good," Vasily said, leaning forward. "You see, my plan isn't simply to repair old buildings and make them look nice." He pointed proudly at the largest map on the wall. "No, it will be a complete renaissance of the Kiev-Pechersk Monastery. It will become a world-renowned spiritual center. By the way," Vasily added with sudden superiority, "have you ever visited the Louvre?"

Tony shook his head. Vasily smiled inwardly—of course, Tony hadn't been to the Louvre, he thought. But he himself had visited it and could, therefore, feel superior.

"Compared to what we'll build here, the Louvre will look like a provincial village," Vasily declared with excitement. He pointed eagerly at the map again. "Here, we'll reconstruct the original printing house—turn it into the best publishing house in the world!"

Tony smiled slightly as Vasily's excitement contorted his face into a strange grimace.

"And here," Vasily continued passionately, "we'll build the Temple of Peace. A sacred place for people of any nationality, religion, or belief to pray to God."

Tony looked puzzled. "Which God exactly?"

"Any God," Vasily said simply.

"So you're saying Muslims, Jews, and Christians would pray together in your temple?" Tony asked skeptically.

"Exactly! I have already discussed this with religious leaders," Vasily insisted.

"But Vasily," Tony said slowly, "they can't even peacefully share Jerusalem. Do you really think they'll suddenly reconcile their differences here overnight? It's impossible. Wars like those in the Middle East would sooner erupt inside your temple than peace."

Tony spoke softly, almost as if thinking aloud, but Vasily clearly heard the doubt in his words. Annoyed, he shot back, "You don't understand! This temple will be unique, built in such a way it will seem suspended between earth and heaven. There will be nothing else like it anywhere in the world. Don't you see how amazing that is?"

He thrust an album of architectural sketches into Tony's hands. Tony glanced through it curiously. "It's beautiful and impressive," he admitted.

"You see!" Vasily cried triumphantly. But his satisfaction vanished with Tony's next words.

"Still, I don't see anything truly spiritual here. This temple seems more like a political symbol or perhaps a museum of world religions—not a genuine temple. There's a huge difference." Tony set the album aside, thoughtful.

Anger surged in Vasily. Who was this American to criticize his life's dream? He shot Vera a resentful glance—had she brought Tony here just to mock him?

Quickly regaining his composure, Vasily continued. "We'll also turn this street into a pedestrian zone, with underground tunnels for cars. But to explain properly, I need my other maps. Let's go to my apartment—it's nearby."

Minutes later, Tony stood shocked inside Vasily's shabby one-room apartment. Despite expensive statues and ancient maps scattered carelessly among beer bottles and overflowing ashtrays, the place was neglected and dreary.

Vasily tugged out an old map from under the worn sofa, spreading it proudly before Tony. "See? A thousand years ago, there wasn't even a road here!"

Tony was distracted by a costly statue next to an empty beer bottle. "Vasily, you could sell just one of these items and buy a new apartment—this place doesn't match someone of your stature."

Vasily angrily brushed away Tony's suggestion. "You think I can't afford better? I've built dozens of apartments for friends and employees!"

"Maybe your sister deserves one, too," Vera teased gently. "Especially with March eighth coming—Women's Day."

Vasily waved her off irritably. "Your apartment will be next to mine, overlooking the monastery! People from all over the world will envy us!"

Tony examined the map carefully. "Wait a minute. Are you planning luxury apartments on monastery territory? So, all your spiritual talk is just a mask to hide a purely commercial project?"

"We need money to fund the monastery's renovation!" Vasily snapped defensively.

Tony fell silent, disappointed. He had believed Vasily genuinely cared about preserving Ukrainian history, but beneath the surface was a man driven solely by money. Yet, Tony thought bitterly, perhaps that would make it easier to persuade Vasily about Saint Antony's tomb—after all, money was Vasily's true motivation.

Chapter 27

After leaving Vasily's apartment, they decided to grab something to eat at a nearby restaurant. Tony listened closely to Vera and Vasily, waiting for just the right moment to bring up the topic that was burning inside him.

Vasily leaned back comfortably in his chair, watching people play billiards at a nearby table.

"Your America is like one giant McDonald's," he smirked. "Everywhere you go, hamburgers and fries. Look at how amazing the food is here—you won't find anything like this back in your country."

"You've got it wrong," Tony replied. "America has plenty of fancy restaurants, just like everywhere else."

"Oh, give me a break," Vasily waved his hand dismissively. "Admit it—you've never eaten anything better than Ukrainian cuisine. Try it; it'll blow your mind."

The waiter brought out their food. Tony's attention drifted to the billiard table. "That's an interesting table. I've never seen one quite like that. It kinda reminds me of a pool table, but the pockets are way smaller, and the balls are bigger."

"That's because it's the real deal," Vasily declared, biting into his burger. "At first, it seems harder because of the big table, large balls, and tiny pockets. But once you get the hang of it, you'll realize that American pool is just child's play. There was a true billiard, called French billiard, that stayed in Europe. You Americans settled for the watered-down version."

"What's that supposed to mean?" Tony shot back, getting annoyed.

"What's hard to understand?" Vasily insisted. "Big tables aren't practical—they take up space, and bar owners wanted quick money. So they shrank the table, widened the pockets, and made smaller balls that even a blind man could sink. They dumbed it down for amateurs, and that's exactly how you Americans handle everything."

Tony's irritation flared. "If you Ukrainians are so smart, why are you still so far behind? America is a great country—the greatest! Everyone else is trying to be like us. You say pool's inferior to billiards? Then why is there a pool table with people playing it right here in your 'fancy' restaurant?"

Vasily snorted with disdain. "It's there for tourists like you."

"Oh yeah? And did you build Chernobyl for tourists too?" Tony snapped. "What about Kiev's water supply? I read online that Kiev used to have real winters and summers, but you flooded the beautiful land and changed the climate. Now it's just slush and rain."

"The climate's the climate," Vasily muttered defensively.

"Really?" Tony pressed on, voice sharp. "If you're all so smart, why didn't you notice the dam was built above the level of the city? That dam is barely holding together now, like everything else around here. If it breaks, half of Kiev will be underwater! American newspapers report how dangerous it is, but you guys ignore it and keep building there. So tell me again—who's really obsessed with money, Americans or Ukrainians?"

"You sure did your homework for someone who just landed here," Vasily replied sarcastically, visibly irritated. "But your information is pretty one-sided. This country looks different from the inside."

"Guys, enough already!" Vera interrupted, exasperated. "Stop arguing like kids."

For a tense moment, silence hung over the table.

Finally, Tony spoke up again. "Vasily, do you have enough connections to help me get permission for an archaeological dig in the Near Caves?"

Vasily's face hardened. "Vera mentioned you wanted to dig up Saint Antony's grave, but I honestly thought it was just some stupid joke. Tony, I'm here to rebuild the monastery, not raid tombs. There's a big difference. Count me out."

Abruptly, Vasily got up from the table.

"Where's he off to?" Tony asked in surprise.

"Outside, probably to smoke," Vera replied calmly. "He'll cool off in a minute. Don't worry. So, what do you think of my brother?"

"He's quite a character," Tony smiled, shifting closer to Vera. "All that arm-waving, the grand gestures. You two seem alike but completely different."

"Of course we're different," Vera said playfully. "I'm a woman."

"Not just any woman. The most beautiful, incredible woman I've ever met."

She laughed softly. Tony leaned in, gently kissing the tips of her fingers.

Oh well, he thought. *If Vasily won't help, no big deal—I've got someone else to talk to.*

Chapter 28

Early the next morning, Vladimir's sleek black Mercedes pulled up smoothly in front of Tony's hotel. Vladimir greeted him warmly, his handshake firm and confident. Tony noticed Vladimir's immaculate appearance—a tailored suit, shining Italian shoes, and subtle yet expensive jewelry. Everything about him screamed wealth and elegance.

It took only about an hour to reach the vodka factory, located just outside Kiev. The factory was an unassuming structure—a plain, gray concrete building surrounded by rusted fences. Its humble exterior stood in stark contrast to Vladimir's flashy persona and luxurious vehicle.

As they entered the factory, the sharp, biting smell of pure alcohol hit Tony immediately, causing him to wrinkle his nose. The air inside was cold and clinical, fluorescent lights flickered overhead, casting pale reflections on the metal tanks and conveyor belts. Bottles clinked rhythmically as they moved along the production line, filling the space with an almost hypnotic sound. The machinery hummed monotonously, workers silently moved between the equipment, focused and indifferent.

Vladimir seemed entirely out of place amidst the industrial simplicity, yet he moved effortlessly, a king surveying his kingdom. He gestured grandly with his hands, his voice smooth and calm yet subtly authoritative.

"Tony, my friend," Vladimir began, placing a hand lightly but purposefully on Tony's shoulder. "This is exactly what you've been searching for. A renaissance of Ukrainian culture through our vodka. We call it Slavic! By promoting Ukrainian vodka worldwide, we are bringing attention back to our rich heritage and traditions."

Tony nodded thoughtfully, intrigued yet hesitant. From the corner of his eye, he noticed Oksana. She stood slightly behind Vladimir, smiling sweetly, but Tony caught a fleeting tension in her eyes.

The director of the factory approached with polite enthusiasm, nervously fussing around Vladimir and his guests. As they moved deeper into the building, Vladimir's smooth voice continued its reassuring pitch.

"Imagine it, Tony," Vladimir said, tightening his grip slightly on Tony's shoulder and guiding him forward. "This isn't just vodka—it's a healing elixir brewed according to ancient, secret recipes that we've discovered in centuries-old manuscripts. Of course," he chuckled lightly, his voice dipping slightly, "it's not something you'd pour in a kid's juice box. But for adults, taken in moderation, it even has health benefits."

Vladimir flashed a charming smile, but Tony felt a faint ripple of unease beneath Vladimir's carefully constructed friendliness. Something in Vladimir's manner reminded him of a high-stakes poker player—a guy who could bluff effortlessly, never revealing his hand until it was too late.

Tony paused thoughtfully, scratching his chin. "Well, Vladimir, it's tempting—but I've gotta say, alcohol isn't exactly healthy food. I'd need some time to think it over. It might be good money, but I'm not sure this aligns with what I'm looking for."

For a brief moment, Vladimir's eyes flashed coldly, but the smile returned almost instantly. "Tony, relax! You Americans worry too much," he said lightly. "Believe me, there's no safer investment. Vodka sells itself—especially ours. Ask Rustam—he'll tell you we've never had an unhappy investor."

Rustam nodded silently. Tony noticed Oksana quickly glance away, her polite smile faltering slightly before she managed to recover it.

Feeling Vladimir's expectant gaze, Tony decided to shift gears. Leaning closer, he lowered his voice. "Listen, Vladimir. Actually, I've got a business idea of my own that might interest you."

Vladimir raised an eyebrow, clearly intrigued. "Really? I always like hearing good ideas—especially from smart people."

"Let's step aside," Vladimir continued smoothly, steering Tony toward a quieter corner away from the others. "You have my full attention. Tell me more."

As Tony began explaining, Vladimir listened attentively, his eyes calm yet calculating as if already assessing how he could turn Tony's idea to his advantage. Tony felt a twinge of doubt again but brushed it off, convincing himself this was merely the normal caution of doing business abroad.

***

It was late evening by the time Tony got back to his hotel. Vladimir gave the Americans a firm handshake as they said their goodbyes.

"Don't worry, Tony," Vladimir assured him. "We'll get the lowdown on this whole archaeological excavation at the monastery. It won't be a cakewalk, but we'll pull every string we've got to help. Too bad you didn't tell me about it sooner."

Tony smiled gratefully. "I appreciate that. Glad you're on board."

"No need for thanks yet. Let's wait until the job's done." Vladimir nodded toward Oksana. "She'll walk you up to your room."

Gracefully, Oksana stepped out of the Mercedes, giving Tony a friendly smile. "We never leave our friends hanging, especially in a city they don't know."

She gently took Tony by the arm, leading him toward the hotel entrance. Vladimir and Rustam stayed by the car, speaking quietly, their eyes following the pair until they vanished through the hotel's revolving doors.

"So, what do you think?" Vladimir asked, lighting a cigarette and inhaling deeply.

Rustam clenched his jaw, eyes narrowed. "He's an odd one, that's for sure."

"You think there's really something buried in that grave?"

Rustam gave an indifferent shrug. "Who gives a damn? Let him cough up the cash first. That's what matters. If we do find something down there, we'll figure out how to split it later."

Vladimir exhaled a thin stream of smoke. "And what about all this talk of curses, all these old wives' tales about doom if someone opens the grave?"

"Superstitious nonsense," Rustam scoffed. "My ancestors razed Kiev to the ground on December 6, 1240—where was the curse then? If the city itself didn't bring bad luck, why would some old bones?"

Vladimir chuckled dryly. "I see your history lessons weren't wasted."

"Five years sitting next to you in university had to pay off sometime," Rustam said, cracking a smile.

"Except your ancestors got their butts kicked out of Kiev in 1362," Vladimir teased.

"You mean when Ukraine rolled over for Lithuania like a submissive woman?" Rustam smirked contemptuously. "Mark my words: soon enough, there'll be more swords than crosses in Kiev. We ruled this city once, and we'll do it again. Slavics understand two things—money and the whip. And lucky for us, we've got both."

Vladimir's smile faded. He took another drag and said nothing more.

***

Tony and Oksana climbed the hotel's elegant staircase, her fingers lazily tracing the intricate carvings of the banister. Tony felt uneasy, unsure how to politely send her on her way.

"Oksana, care for a drink or something?" he offered, just to break the tension.

She smiled warmly, leaning into him just enough to blur the line between casual and intimate. "I thought you'd never ask."

Tony glanced down at the sparkling engagement ring on her finger. "It's pretty late. Won't your fiancé mind?"

She laughed softly, tilting her head with playful defiance. "Even if he did, what's the worst that could happen? He works for Vladimir. Trust me—he knows when to look the other way."

Tony felt his pulse quicken. Her closeness made him nervous and exhilarated all at once. She lightly touched his wrist, sending an electric current straight through him.

"So tell me, Tony," Oksana whispered, stepping even closer, "do you like Kiev?"

"It's a beautiful city," Tony replied absently, his voice coming out quieter than he'd intended.

She lifted her eyes to his, teasingly biting her lower lip. "You have no idea how breathtaking Kiev can be after dark. I can show you, if you want..."

Tony's gaze drifted down to her mouth—temptingly close, inviting him. He hesitated, caught between desire and doubt. His mind flashed to Vera, and a pang of guilt twisted in his chest.

"Maybe...I shouldn't," he murmured, more to himself than to her, even as his body betrayed him.

"Come on, Tony," Oksana coaxed softly, her voice silky and irresistible. "Life's short. Why not live a little?"

Tony's eyes lingered on Oksana's lips. He hesitated.

Chapter 29

Vasily often worked late into the night. Tonight, he was still in his office, shuffling through piles of papers scattered across his desk. The building was quiet, so when he heard footsteps in the hallway, he paused and glanced up, wondering who could possibly be there at this hour.

The door swung open, and Vera entered the office.

"You're still working?" she asked, or perhaps simply stated the obvious, as she settled into the leather couches across from him.

"Oh, sis... Hey!" Vasily leaned back, raising an eyebrow at her stylish appearance. "Where are you heading, all dressed up? And where's your American?"

Vera crossed her legs casually. "He left this morning with some businessmen to visit a vodka factory," she said, glancing briefly at her watch. "Still hasn't returned, though. He promised to call as soon as he got back."

Vasily chuckled, shaking his head. "I can only imagine what condition they'll bring him back in after touring a vodka plant."

Seeing the troubled look on Vera's face, he softened slightly. "Come on, don't get upset."

"I'm not upset," Vera replied glumly, her eyes lowered.

"All Americans are the same, Vera," Vasily said dismissively. "They have nothing but dollars rattling around in their heads."

"Not all," Vera said firmly. She raised her gaze, meeting her brother's eyes. "You're wrong about a lot of things, Vasily. Maybe it's you who still can't decide what matters more—money or spirituality."

Vasily bristled at this but had no interest in arguing with his sister. Instead, he steered the conversation in a different direction. "So what's new at the monastery?"

"You're there practically every day; don't you already know?" Vera gave him a meaningful look. "Strange things have started happening. The monks are afraid to go down into the caves again."

Vasily put down his pen. "Afraid? Why?"

"They say the Black Monk has begun appearing again."

Vasily stared at his sister, surprised she'd even say something like that. "Come on, Vera. It's just a legend—there's no proof of it, nothing historical at all. Personally, I only believe facts."

Vera looked at her brother reproachfully. "You're saying you only believe in what you can touch?"

"Not exactly," Vasily countered, slightly irritated. "But this Black Monk story is just superstition. One monk sees another monk in the shadows and imagines it's the Black Monk. Big deal. They all dress the same—black robes, black hair, black beards."

"But they see each other every day," Vera insisted. "And they know the caves better than we know our own homes. No," she shook her head slowly, "something's off."

Vasily's expression turned serious. "So how often is he supposed to appear?"

"That's the thing. Very rarely—just a handful of times over the past thousand years. And always just before something terrible happens. The monks say the Black Monk warns of impending tragedy. The last sighting was eighty years ago."

Vasily considered this. "Right before the Revolution, Civil War, World War Two... Are you saying this ghost is some kind of messenger?"

"Who said anything about a ghost?" Vera said softly.

Vasily raised his eyebrows. "If not a ghost, then what?"

Vera didn't answer immediately. Her eyes stared through him, unfocused, lost somewhere distant. The intensity in her gaze unsettled Vasily.

"You mean someone's been living secretly in the catacombs for a thousand years, or a corpse walks out of his tomb from time to time?" Vasily scoffed nervously.

Vera's silence hung heavily in the air.

"Whatever it is," Vasily said finally, trying to dispel the unease, "its appearances before tragedies could simply be coincidences."

"Maybe," Vera finally spoke, breaking the tension. "But there's another strange detail in the legend. The Black Monk only appears at Saint Anthony's tomb and only when someone carrying his blood comes to the Near Caves."

Vasily lit a cigar, blowing smoke thoughtfully. "Come on, Vera. Anthony couldn't have had descendants—he was a monk! He never touched women, never had children."

Vera smiled faintly. "You're right. He didn't have children, but he could've had relatives like anyone else. And about women..." she brushed back a strand of her hair and continued softly, "Can anyone really know for sure what happened a thousand years ago?"

Vasily eyed her carefully. "Are you seriously suggesting the founder of the greatest monastery in all Kievan Rus wasn't celibate?"

Vera shrugged slightly. "Saint Anthony lived a strict, ascetic life, but he wasn't a monk in today's sense. He was flesh and blood, just like us."

Vasily flicked cigar ash onto a scrap of paper. "Vera, what's bothering you? What's really on your mind?"

Vera glanced down at the cell phone she'd been holding anxiously. Tony still hadn't called. She looked back at her brother. "In his will, Saint Anthony explicitly forbade anyone from disturbing his grave."

"And?" Vasily shrugged. "Lots of people don't want their graves disturbed. There's nothing odd about it." Then Vasily remembered how differently burials were treated a thousand years ago—more serious, more sacred. Today, bodies are burned or quickly buried without ceremony.

Suddenly, a strange note in Vera's voice caught Vasily's attention. Was she thinking about how her own parents had been buried? He watched her closely. Yet Vera seemed calm and composed, as if discussing something impersonal.

"According to Byzantine tradition," Vera continued evenly, "a monk's tomb would be opened exactly one year after burial.

Saint Anthony knew that. Yet he suddenly broke tradition, explicitly forbidding it. Why?"

The melodic ringing of a cell phone interrupted their conversation. Vera glanced down, her expression instantly brightening. "It's Tony! I have to go!" She jumped up, flashing a quick smile. "Don't work too late, okay?"

Before Vasily could respond, she'd already vanished through the open doorway, leaving only a lingering trace of perfume behind.

Vasily stared at the empty doorway, then glanced at the clock. An unpleasant wave of jealousy rolled through him. Yes, Vera was his adopted sister, and yes, he loved her dearly and wanted only the best for her. But even so, Vasily couldn't shake the disturbing feeling that had long haunted him. He rarely admitted it, even to himself, but deep inside, he wanted her as a woman.

Chapter 30

It took Tony considerable effort to finally get rid of Oksana. The moment the door closed behind the persistent translator, he picked up the phone and called Vera.

Vera had become the center of his universe—other women no longer existed for him. They talked late into the evening, their conversation easy and comforting. Afterward, Tony returned to his hotel room and fell swiftly into bed, drifting into sleep.

Despite the wonderful evening, Tony's sleep was restless, his dreams thick and oppressive, dragging him downward like a current of heavy tar.

In the dream, Tony stood in an empty square before the Kiev-Pechersk Lavra. The sky hung low, a dark, leaden canopy pressing down on the city. Thick banks of fog crawled along the

ground like ghostly shadows, wrapping around his ankles and holding him firmly in place.

A sudden sharp crack echoed through the air. Tony lifted his eyes in alarm, watching the enormous cross atop the dome of the All Saints Church slowly tilt as if some invisible giant hand pressed down upon it. Another cracking sound, louder this time—and the cross toppled violently, splintering into countless fragments against the stone pavement. The acrid smell of burning wood mingled with the unmistakable metallic tang of fresh blood.

Tony stood frozen in horror, unable to move. A mob of hooded strangers surged past him, pouring into the monastery gates. Their faces were obscured, but their eyes glowed with fury and fanaticism. Laughing wildly, they ripped ancient relics from the walls, trampled sacred books underfoot, and shattered everything in their path. Tony tried to shout and try to stop them, but his voice vanished, leaving only helpless silence.

Abruptly, the scene shifted. Tony found himself inside an ancient cathedral, bathed in dim, red light. All around him were coffins—dozens, hundreds—arranged in solemn rows. They lay open, revealing soldiers in military uniforms, their pale faces frozen in expressions of agony. Limp arms hung from the sides of the coffins, lifeless fingers brushing the cold stone floor.

Amid this grim assembly, oblivious to the dead beneath their feet, young men danced feverishly, intoxicated by drugs and alcohol. Eyes burning with madness, their distorted faces bore grotesque smiles as they stumbled over corpses without pause, locked in an ecstatic, nightmarish dance.

The vision strangled Tony, gripping his throat with invisible, steel fingers. He fought desperately to wake up, yet his body refused to obey. Each attempt to escape only plunged him deeper into darkness.

Images flashed past in rapid succession, merging into a haunting kaleidoscope. Like shards of a shattered mirror, each fragment reflected a distorted, horrifying reality.

Then, abruptly, silence fell. No voices, no whispers, not even a breath—just profound, unnerving stillness. Tony felt himself pulled slowly but irresistibly into the depths of time, passing through layers of mist and shadow until he emerged into an age long past.

A dense, ancient forest appeared before him, illuminated only faintly by a pale moon. A narrow path climbed uphill into the heart of the darkness, exuding a sinister yet irresistible force. Along this path moved a lone figure—a man cloaked in a long, black robe, his hood concealing his features. He walked calmly, deliberately, certain of his path. Each footstep left a faint trace in the dew, the earth greedily absorbing and preserving his passage.

Something rustled in the undergrowth, accompanied by a wary howl. Wolf-like shadows darted between the trees, drawing closer, but the monk showed no fear. He knew they would not attack, sensing the ancient power that radiated from him. His worry was not the beasts but something heavier—the crushing weight of human suffering. The endless cruelty and pain that people inflicted upon one another were a burden he could hardly bear.

Pausing, the monk raised his head toward the sky hidden by dense branches. His lips moved silently, whispering a prayer that sent invisible vibrations through the air. Suddenly, as though sensing Tony's presence across centuries, the monk turned sharply and stared directly at him. Tony recoiled. The monk's eyes were black, bottomless wells of sorrow and wisdom—eyes that had witnessed far too much.

An unsettling realization flashed clearly into Tony's mind: perhaps the land's fertility and beauty came not from nature alone, nor from rivers or fields, but from centuries of pain and suffering, generously watered by the blood and tears of those who lived and died here.

Far below, through the trees, the tranquil surface of the Dnieper shimmered softly as if guarding something immense and ancient in its depths—something better left undisturbed. Yet the monk knew peace had already been shattered; soon, the earth would tremble with screams of anguish.

Too often people try to glimpse the future, longing to know what tomorrow, next year, or the next century holds—never considering how heavy such knowledge might be. How agonizing to watch tragedies unfold, powerless to intervene, reduced to a mere observer whose heart breaks with helplessness.

The monk drew a deep breath of cold night air, letting its damp bitterness fill his lungs. The forest lay still, the wolves silenced, acknowledging the gravity of the moment. Here, on this ancient hill, time had halted for him. This land held tight to those who dared touch its mysteries; every tree and stone preserved memories and echoed voices from the past. Now, he, too, was forever bound to this timeless place.

His heart ached with sorrow. Ahead lay centuries of war and bloodshed, armies treading the soil and leaving ashes and graves in their wake. This future was already written, its cruel lines etched clearly into his soul by a hand soaked in blood.

No one knew Saint Anthony's true name. Some believed he was born in the town of Liubech during the reign of Grand Prince Vladimir Sviatoslavich; others said he had come from distant lands, driven by an unknown purpose. His birth name was lost forever, dissolved into the mist of the past.

He traveled widely, visiting sacred places, absorbing ancient traditions. In Greece, on the holy Mount Athos, he accepted monastic tonsure, taking the name Anthony. From then onward, this name inspired awe and reverence—some regarded him as a prophet and saint, others feared him, aware of his ability to perceive the hidden truths of human souls.

In 1013, Anthony returned to his homeland. Near Kiev, atop a secluded hill, he dug a cave and withdrew into prayer and strict asceticism. But peace eluded him. News of the mysterious hermit spread swiftly, drawing pilgrims seeking guidance and blessings. They called him Anthony of Pechersk, from the word 'pechera, ' meaning cave. Some even named him a prophet, believing him capable of foretelling future events.

It was a troubled era for Rus'. Grand Prince Vladimir Sviatoslavich struggled with rebellions and conspiracies. His son Yaroslav, ruling Novgorod, defied his father, refusing tribute to Kiev. Vladimir, aged and exhausted, died mysteriously in 1015, plunging his sons into bloody conflict.

After Vladimir's death, Sviatopolk, later named "the Accursed," seized Kiev, ruthlessly ordering the deaths of his brothers Boris and Gleb—the first innocent blood spilled in this dynastic strife. Rumors claimed Sviatopolk also sought the death of a mysterious monk living near Kiev, but Anthony forewarned, escaped again to Greece, avoiding imminent peril.

Rus' descended into civil war. For four bitter years, Yaroslav fought Sviatopolk, bolstered by Novgorodians, Varangian warriors, and allies from distant Sweden—the homeland of his wife, Ingegerda. Sviatopolk, desperate, allied with Poles and the Pecheneg nomads—Rus' ancient enemies.

In 1019, in the decisive battle by the Alta River, Sviatopolk suffered defeat and died in flight, abandoned in a foreign land, restless in death.

What had Yaroslav felt upon hearing of his brother's demise? Relief at victory and peace, or anguish at memories of childhood days together in their father's palace? Could anyone truly rejoice, knowing the heavy price paid for power?

In 1051, after thirty-six years of exile, Anthony returned once more to Kiev. From the hilltop, he gazed at the Dnieper, watching the river carry away memories of countless lives. Perhaps he reflected that life was as fleeting as the river's current—uncertain and ever-changing. Or perhaps he pondered the inexorable march of time, which, eventually, would erase distinctions between princes and hermits, conquerors and supplicants, saints and sinners alike, dissolving their names forever into eternity.

Chapter 31

Vladimir leaned back lazily in his chair, looking across at Tony with mild amusement. "We checked everything out," he began, nodding toward Rustam, who stood silently by the window. "As a foreigner, you can't officially get permission for an archaeological dig at the Kiev-Pechersk Monastery. Even if you were Ukrainian, you'd still hit a brick wall. Trust me, you'd burn through a lot of time and cash and still end up empty-handed."

Tony glanced curiously at Rustam. "So that's it? No options at all?"

Vladimir exchanged a quick look with Rustam and smiled. "Not exactly. See, we're not in America, Tony—we're in Ukraine." Vladimir leaned forward slightly, his voice lowering as if sharing a secret. "Saint Anthony is buried in handmade catacombs, right? Built by monks about a thousand years ago. After all this time, it's obvious these catacombs urgently need repairs."

His lips curled into a sly grin. "We start renovation works there, strictly to preserve our beloved historical site, you understand. But suddenly, quite by accident, we uncover Anthony's grave.

What a surprise! And, of course, who could've prevented it? It's nobody's fault." Vladimir chuckled softly. "You catch my drift?"

Tony nodded slowly, processing Vladimir's words. Vladimir leaned back again, casually checking his expensive wristwatch. "Good. Now, if we're clear on this, let's talk money."

The clock struck noon.

***

At the same time, Vasily stopped by the Kiev-Pechersk Monastery on business and decided to visit his sister.

"That suit looks great on you," Vera remarked casually as they passed by the golden domes of the Assumption Cathedral. Sunlight shimmered gently across the polished stone pavement, filling the monastery grounds with a soft glow.

"I had it custom-made," Vasily replied proudly, brushing imaginary dust off the sleeve. "Italian fabric—only the best."

He always enjoyed it when someone noticed his impeccable taste. Vasily carefully followed fashion, savoring his image of wealth and sophistication.

They walked on in silence for a few moments until Vasily finally broke it with a sly, provocative smile.

"You know, Vera, there's just one thing I can't wrap my head around. What do you actually see in this American?"

Vera slowed her pace, irritation already beginning to flare up inside her. She tried to control her voice, but her brother always knew exactly how to strike a nerve.

"How can I even explain it to you?" she replied softly. "He's just… a genuinely good person, Vasia."

A mocking smirk appeared on Vasily's face. He stopped theatrically, pressing one hand dramatically to his chest.

"Oh, Vera! You almost made a grown man cry! Did you finally get tired of all our local guys? Now you've decided to pick up some foreigner? Not exactly something to brag about, you know."

Vera stopped abruptly, turning to face him directly. Her eyes flashed angrily.

"Oh, and walking out on your wife and child—now that's something to brag about? Or chasing after every cheap hooker you see—is that considered normal? Maybe decent girls just won't give you the time of day anymore."

Vasily's face darkened instantly. He raised his voice, cutting her off sharply:

"We're not talking about me right now, Vera. We're talking about you. My life's stable—what about yours? You can't even hold down a relationship for more than a few weeks! Tell me, did you manage to convince your American that you're some innocent little virgin? Out of all the men in this country, not one is good enough for you?"

"Show me one decent man!" Vera shot back, practically shouting. Anger had overtaken her completely. "Just look around! Either they're perverts or total mama's boys. Those who seem smart are so caught up in their own little worlds that they forget to shower or change their socks!"

She stepped closer, glaring fiercely into her brother's eyes.

"And the rest—like your so-called 'business partners'? They are just greedy bastards who steal from everyone and then brag about their money as if they earned it. They're pathetic, weak men, Vasily. I'd rather spend the rest of my life alone than waste even a minute on guys like that."

Vasily's jaw tightened; she'd clearly hit a nerve, though he tried to mask it. He flung out a hand dismissively, attempting to brush her words away.

"Oh, sure! And your precious Tony is some kind of knight in shining armor, right? All his American dollars must've really swept you off your feet!"

"I don't give a damn about his money!" Vera's voice cracked with rage and pain. "Plenty of your friends have even more than Tony, but have you ever seen me give a second glance to any of them?"

Vasily leaned closer, lowering his voice to an angry whisper.

"Wake up, Vera. This American is just your ticket out of here. He'd be an idiot not to grab a Ukrainian beauty like you, marry you, and drag you back to America. But once he's back in Chicago, he'll forget you even existed. You're nothing but a short adventure for him—don't be naive."

Tears burned Vera's eyes, but she refused to let them fall. The quiet chants from pilgrims echoed softly around them, making their heated exchange seem even more bitter and painful.

"You know what, Vasily? I don't interfere in your life, so stop meddling in mine." Her voice was quiet but firm. "And for your information, I'm not going anywhere. Certainly not to America. Do you understand me?"

For a long moment, Vasily just stood there, studying her. Finally, he shrugged coldly.

"Fine, Vera. Do whatever the hell you want. Just don't come crying to me later."

He spun around sharply, leaving her standing alone as he marched out of the monastery grounds, disappearing into the warm afternoon haze.

Chapter 32

Tony paced nervously back and forth in his hotel room, his phone pressed tightly to his ear. Outside, the evening lights of Kiev glimmered softly through the blinds. He was already beginning to regret making the call, but now it was too late.

"Michael, listen—I need money, and I need it fast."

Silence hung heavily on the line, lingering longer than Tony could bear.

"Michael, you still there?"

On the other end, Michael rubbed his forehead wearily, gazing out at the Chicago skyline from his top-floor office. After nearly twenty years in the financial industry, he trusted numbers far more than intuition. Right now, however, Tony's tone was setting off every alarm in his mind.

"Tony, what the hell's going on? Tell me straight—are you in trouble over there? I warned you about diving headfirst into investments without proper due diligence. Ukraine isn't exactly risk-free."

Tony groaned, waving his hand impatiently as though Michael could somehow see his frustration. "Come on, man, this isn't about investments. It's personal. I'm asking you, as a friend, to trust me and lend me some money. No paperwork, nothing official. You know I'm good for it."

Michael leaned back heavily in his chair, feeling his stomach tighten. His instincts, honed by years of high-stakes decisions, screamed at him to walk away. But Tony wasn't just a friend—he was practically family. Abandoning him now would leave a bitter taste.

"Look, Tony, I get it. But you have to understand, something about this feels off."

"If I wasn't sure about it, I wouldn't be calling," Tony cut him off, irritation creeping into his voice. "When have I ever let you down?"

Michael hesitated, tapping his pen anxiously against the desk. "Damn it, Tony. You're really twisting my arm here. Alright, fine. Where do I send the money?"

"I'll email you the account details," Tony replied quickly, relief washing over him.

Michael immediately tensed up again. "Whose account, exactly?"

"It's clean, Mike. A local firm with a solid reputation. These guys are legit—they've got serious connections over here. Nothing sketchy."

Behind Tony, a shadow silently slipped through the hotel wall, stopping mere inches from his shoulder—watching quietly, motionless, patient as fate itself.

Michael exhaled slowly. There was desperation in Tony's voice, and Michael knew better than anyone just how stubborn his friend could be.

"Jesus, Tony, you really don't give up, do you? But listen, if anything smells fishy, I'm pulling the plug immediately, understood?"

"Absolutely. Trust me, it's important," Tony insisted, pacing again. His gaze landed on his grandfather's photograph on the table, and a sudden sadness gripped him.

"By the way," Michael said, his tone softening, "I ran into Sofia yesterday. She's worried—says you've completely dropped off the radar. She called your hotel at least a dozen times. Are you avoiding her?"

Tony's chest tightened painfully. Hearing Sofia's name shattered his composure, catching him off guard. He hadn't expected her absence to hit him this hard. For a moment, he stood frozen, caught between the past he'd left behind and the uncertain future he'd stepped into.

"Tony? You still there?"

"Yeah," Tony said hoarsely, swallowing hard. "Thanks, Mike. I'll call her soon."

But as he hung up, Tony realized he wouldn't make that call— at least, not yet. He slowly turned back toward his grandfather's picture, his eyes tracing the familiar lines of the old man's face.

"Why the hell didn't we talk more, Grandpa?" he whispered bitterly, as though the photograph might somehow answer. Regret stung his throat. It was cruel how clearly everything came into focus once people were gone. He'd spent his entire life pushing the old man away, always too busy, too distracted, too sure there'd be time later.

But later, it had come and gone, leaving behind only silence.

Tony reached out, lightly touching the cold glass of the frame.

"Come on, Grandpa, give me something—anything. Tell me what I'm supposed to do now. I could really use your advice."

But the room remained quiet.

Chapter 33

Vera sat curled up on the couch, watching the sunset spill gently through the hotel curtains. She had come to pick Tony up and show him the quiet beauty of Kiev, but somehow, her plans had scattered along with her clothes across the floor. Before she fully realized what was happening, she found herself lost in Tony's embrace.

Tony softly brushed a strand of hair away from Vera's face. "You have such beautiful eyes," he whispered, tracing her eyebrows gently. "And your hair…and your hands," he murmured, pressing his lips tenderly to each fingertip.

Vera laughed softly, turning her face away to hide the blush rising to her cheeks. "I'm just glad you fell in love with Kiev," she said quietly, her voice warm and sincere. "It's your land, you know. Even if you've never lived here, it's yours. Maybe it doesn't glitter like Chicago, maybe it doesn't have the comforts you're used to—but there's a warmth here, Tony. It's a warmth that can hold you together when nothing else will."

He smiled, gently cupping her face in his hands. "You know what? I could kiss these hands of yours all day long."

Vera laughed again, pushing him playfully away. "Oh, come on! You're such a liar," she teased affectionately, her eyes sparkling. Yet, deep inside, she felt like the most desired, happiest woman on earth. The intensity of his gaze sent a shiver through her heart. But something still gnawed quietly inside her chest.

She carefully searched his face, suddenly becoming serious. "Tony, I'm relieved you've finally given up on your crazy idea of opening Saint Anthony's grave. I still can't even imagine how such a thought ever crossed your mind."

Tony looked away, avoiding her probing gaze. Silence filled the room, the playful warmth quickly draining away.

"What is it?" Vera asked, sitting up. Her voice was now tinged with uncertainty. "What are you thinking about? Or rather—who are you thinking about? Other women?" Her tone held a teasing edge, yet the undertone betrayed her vulnerability.

Tony turned abruptly. "Don't be ridiculous. You're the only woman I can even think about anymore."

He leaned in slowly, their lips nearly touching, when the sudden sharp ring of the phone sliced through their intimacy. Vera flinched, startled, and Tony recoiled instinctively. For a brief moment, they both froze, suspended in uneasy silence as the ringing continued to cut sharply through the fading warmth around them.

Tony stood up slowly, his movements now uncertain. He glanced apologetically toward Vera before picking up the phone, answering with visible hesitation.

"Hello?" he said quietly. His jaw tensed as Vladimir's confident voice filled his ear.

"Tony, the money arrived. Everything is set. If you're ready, we can start the excavation tomorrow morning. We'll wait for your signal."

Tony cast another quick glance at Vera, who was staring at him intently, wrapped only in the soft sheet, her slender silhouette glowing softly against the dimming sunlight. A sudden wave of guilt overcame him. Without fully understanding why, he reached for the small-framed photograph of his grandfather on the bedside table. The old man seemed to watch him silently. Tony hesitated, then quickly placed it back on the table, face down.

"I'll call you back shortly," he muttered abruptly, hanging up.

Vera rose from the couch—graceful, vulnerable, and heartbreakingly beautiful. She took a cautious step toward him, the unease palpable in her voice. "Tony, is everything all right?"

He felt torn, painfully aware of the heat of desire still pulling him toward her, calling him back to their moment of intimacy. It took every ounce of strength he had to resist the impulse. Tony quickly grabbed his pants, avoiding her questioning gaze.

"Everything's fine," he lied smoothly, forcing casualness into his voice. "That was just reception downstairs. They said a fax arrived from the States. I'll go down quickly and pick it up. I'll be right back."

Without looking back at her, Tony hurried from the room, closing the door firmly behind him. Vera remained standing alone, her gaze fixed anxiously on the closed door.

Chapter 34

A faded, rusty sign hung crookedly at the entrance of the monastery catacombs: *"Sorry, but the Middle Caves are closed to visitors due to renovation."* Beside it stood a bored policeman, kicking at loose stones on the ground, watching for anyone who either couldn't read or didn't care about rules.

Farther in, at the shadowy mouth of the tunnels, Tony stood with Vladimir and Rustam, watching silently as workers in reflective vests prepared their drills and lights. Ancient stone walls loomed around them, damp and glistening in the flickering lamplight. The air was heavy, thick with moisture, and had an unmistakable scent of decay and age. Tony's heart pounded with a mix of excitement and unease. In just moments, he might solve a thousand-year-old mystery—one that could change his life forever.

He glanced at Vladimir, who appeared composed as always, his dark eyes calm but dangerously intense. Still, there was a tension in his posture, a subtle eagerness that betrayed his impatience. Rustam stood slightly behind, arms crossed.

A sudden echo of rapid footsteps broke through Tony's thoughts.

"Tony!"

He turned sharply, feeling a chill that had nothing to do with the cavern's temperature. Vera stood there, her face pale and her eyes blazing with urgency, clutching a small leather-bound notebook so tightly her knuckles had turned white.

"Tony, stop! Please! You have to stop this now!" Her voice shook with fear and anger, slicing through the cave's oppressive silence. "If you violate Saint Anthony's tomb, you're violating our entire past, disrespecting every ancestor who's ever lived here! You can't do this! Your grandfather—he would never want this!"

Tony felt a sharp sting of guilt, momentarily paralyzing him. He hesitated, glancing down briefly at the muddy ground.

"Vera," he finally said, forcing himself to sound calm, "it's too late to turn back. You have no idea how much money I've sunk into this just to get this damn 'renovation' approved. This is happening. I can't just stop."

Vera's eyes filled with fury and disbelief. "Do you even hear yourself right now? You sound insane! Even if there are jewels buried down there, they don't belong to you. You're stealing from the dead!"

Tony's patience snapped, his frustration pouring out like acid. "I'm about to be richer than I ever dreamed! What don't you understand?"

Vera stood frozen, looking at Tony as if seeing him clearly for the first time—selfish, greedy, utterly consumed.

"How could I have been so blind?" she whispered bitterly. "If money means this much to you, then take it. Dig up your damned treasure! But if you do, just know this: you will never see me again."

Tony reached for her instinctively, panic rising in his chest. "Vera, listen! I'm doing this for us—this money, it's for our future!"

"Our future?" she laughed bitterly, tears streaming freely down her face now. "You're doing this for yourself. Nothing sacred matters to you. If you can betray your grandfather's memory, why should I think you wouldn't betray me next?"

She turned sharply, leaving Tony staring helplessly into the empty darkness.

Rustam spat on the ground angrily, shaking his head. "Who the hell let that bitch in here?" He walked closer, slapping Tony's shoulder roughly in mock sympathy. "Forget about her. In a few hours, you'll have enough cash to buy any woman in Kiev."

Tony's voice was barely audible as he stared down the empty tunnel. "What about the women who can't be bought?"

Rustam laughed coldly. "Everything can be bought. Even her. You just haven't named the right price yet."

Tony felt nausea rise within him. Vladimir approached silently, placing a firm hand on Tony's shoulder. His eyes glittered in the dim light.

"Don't worry, Tony," he said calmly, his voice deceptively soft yet edged with menace. "When you see what's inside that grave, you'll forget about everything else. We're making history here. You don't want to miss it."

Tony shivered involuntarily, glancing back one last time to where Vera had disappeared. He suddenly felt as if unseen eyes were watching from the darkness, silently condemning him.

Slowly, Vladimir nodded to the workers. The roar of machinery broke through the eerie stillness, a jarring violation of the ancient silence.

Chapter 35

Vera's phone rang sharply, slicing through the silence that filled her apartment. Slowly, as if every movement required enormous strength, she rose from the bed, feeling the cool floor beneath her bare feet. The curtains were drawn carelessly.

She picked up the phone, her hand trembling slightly.

"Vera?" Tony's voice pierced her soul.

Without answering, she tossed the phone onto the bed. It kept ringing, each shrill tone like a fresh wound. Vera sat down again, burying her face into the pillow.

She had believed Tony was different—believed he could become the man she'd always hoped for, someone strong enough to stay with her forever. But it turned out to be nothing but a sweet illusion, a fleeting dream broken by reality. When the ringing finally ceased, the apartment fell into a bitter silence, pressing harder on her heart than any words could have.

Then the doorbell sounded sharply, echoing through the apartment and making her flinch. Vera wiped her tear-streaked cheeks and stood unsteadily. Approaching the door, she hesitated a moment before undoing the chain and pulling it open.

Tony stood in the doorway. Their gazes met, and Vera felt something deep inside her chest tighten painfully.

"Vera," Tony said quietly, his voice filled with remorse. "I—I called it off. I never touched Anthony's grave, didn't desecrate anything. I swear it." He paused, searching for the right words. "None of that treasure matters. You're all that matters. You mean more to me than anything else in this world."

Slowly, almost instinctively, she stepped toward Tony, pressing her cheek against his chest. She could hear his heartbeat, rapid and anxious. She wanted to cry again, but no tears were left inside her—only emptiness remained. Tony wrapped his arms around her tightly, as if afraid she might vanish.

***

Rustam stared thoughtfully at Anthony's tomb, then shot Vladimir a questioning glance.

"Listen, the American chickened out, but he already paid us. Nothing's stopping us from opening the grave ourselves. Let's crack it open, grab whatever's inside, and get the hell out."

Vladimir shifted uneasily; anxiety etched into his face. "Tony wouldn't just bail if he thought something valuable was down there. Americans aren't stupid—they don't throw money around without a reason. He must've learned something, maybe from that girl. You saw how upset she was, yelling at him. She came out of nowhere and left just as quickly. Something's off here..."

Vladimir's voice dropped to a tense whisper as he glanced around nervously, beads of sweat forming on his forehead.

"Maybe... maybe we shouldn't even be down here."

Rustam gave Vladimir a disgusted look. "You're kidding me, right? We're inches from becoming rich. This is a one-in-a-million shot. Five minutes of courage, and we're set for life."

Vladimir swallowed hard, his eyes flickering toward the cave's entrance. "The monks are getting suspicious. They're gathering at the entrance. Pretty soon they'll come down here, figure out no one's actually repairing anything, and then we'll be screwed. Let's get out while we still can. We've got the American's cash. If things go sideways now, we'll lose everything. Let's go!"

Rustam spat on the ground defiantly. "Run if you want, but I'm not leaving empty-handed. Anthony measured this monastery's land with a golden belt, gifted by Shimon, son of Afrikan, the Varangian duke. You think he didn't stash away treasures here? Anthony paid gold to master artisans from Constantinople. Think about the riches that monk had! And now they could belong to me. Do you seriously believe I'd just walk away?"

Rustam turned decisively toward the tomb, then froze. A black shadow stood silently between him and the grave.

A scream erupted from Vladimir's throat, raw and animalistic. Workers scrambled in panic, shoving each other aside as they bolted toward the cave's exit.

Vladimir slipped in his frantic attempt to flee, crashing heavily into a glass relic display. The glass shattered on impact, slicing his face. Blood streamed from his forehead as he shrieked again, crawling desperately into the dark corner of the cave. Shards of broken glass and blood spattered over the tomb's ancient shroud.

Rustam's courage dissolved into panic. Heart pounding, he spun around, sprinting wildly through the cave's twisting tunnels, fueled by instinct alone. The deeper he ran, the darker and narrower the passages became, until suddenly he halted, gasping for breath. Despair closed around his chest like an iron vise. He was utterly alone in the labyrinth, lost, and disoriented.

Fear surged through him, but pride and desperation forced Rustam to steady himself. He took a shaky step forward and nearly tripped over a sledgehammer abandoned by one of the fleeing workers.

"A stroke of luck," Rustam thought, gripping the handle tightly.

He spun around, facing the darkness that seemed alive, watching him. Summoning a desperate bravado, he shouted hoarsely, "Stay back! Whoever you are, I'm warning you—move aside or I'll split your skull open!"

The shadow drew closer, silent and relentless. The outline sharpened into a figure—a monk cloaked entirely in black, his icy eyes piercing straight into Rustam's soul.

With a guttural roar, Rustam swung the sledgehammer at the monk's face with every ounce of strength he had left.

But at the moment of impact, the figure vanished. Rustam's hammer smashed instead into a thick wooden support beam, splintering it violently. He barely had time to register his mistake before a deafening crack filled the tunnel.

The ceiling gave way, crushing down upon him, burying Rustam's final scream beneath an avalanche of stone and darkness.

***

A crowd had already gathered near the entrance to the Near Caves, pushing closer to see what was happening. The faint sound of sirens cut through the anxious murmurs, and blue lights flashed rhythmically against the old monastery walls.

"What on earth happened?" a woman asked shakily, clutching her child's hand.

"Something collapsed down in the caves," an elderly man answered, standing on tiptoe to see over the crowd. "They say someone died."

A young monk stood quietly at the entrance, watching the chaos with an expression of forced calm. Dust covered his robes, and his eyes seemed tired and distant.

"What happened down there, Father?" a tall man asked him sharply.

The monk hesitated a moment, then answered: "There was a collapse in the Near Caves. They were doing some sort of renovation work down there. One of the workers was killed instantly."

A heavy silence fell briefly over the crowd, interrupted by gasps and scattered cries.

"Oh my God," a middle-aged woman whispered, crossing herself repeatedly. "Lord, have mercy!"

"What about the others?" demanded another man, his voice thick with emotion.

"One survived, but…" The monk shook his head slightly, searching for words. "He's lost his mind. He keeps saying he saw Saint Anthony himself."

As he spoke, paramedics emerged from the cave entrance, carefully guiding the shivering, semi-conscious man toward the ambulance. Vladimir's eyes were wide and wild, staring at something no one else could see. His entire body shook with fear, his hands trembling uncontrollably, and dried blood stained his dusty clothes.

"It was him!" Vladimir suddenly shouted, his voice echoing across the monastery courtyard. "Lord, forgive us! He warned us not to disturb his grave!"

"Quiet, quiet," a paramedic murmured, carefully helping him into the ambulance.

The crowd's anxiety surged. People exchanged terrified glances, voices rising louder and more insistent.

The monk sighed deeply, his calm voice contrasting sharply with the crowd's growing hysteria.

"I believe the caves will remain closed for quite a long time after this," he said quietly, turning away.

Chapter 36

Tony quietly sat on the edge of the bed, studying Vera's face as she slept. A soft, fleeting smile touched her lips—like a brief glimpse of sunlight slipping through storm clouds.

Gently, almost reverently, Tony brushed a stray lock of hair away from her cheek, careful not to disturb her rest. He wondered briefly what world she had traveled to and wished desperately that he could follow her there—away from the heavy weight of failure and regret that now pressed down upon him.

Turning toward the window, Tony stood up slowly and gazed out at the sleeping city. Dawn was breaking quietly, spilling pale, golden light over Kiev's rooftops. Yesterday's decisions now loomed over him, darkening every glimmer of hope he'd once had. Michael's money—the loan he'd trusted Tony with—had evaporated into nothing. His dreams of newfound wealth and independence were gone. Tony had gambled and lost, and now his pride lay shattered like glass scattered across the floor.

But even worse than losing the money was the thought of losing Vera. She deserved far more than empty promises and reckless decisions. Tony felt a surge of anxiety twist through his chest as he realized that leaving Ukraine now meant leaving her as well.

What am I supposed to do with Vera? The thought repeated itself like an echo in his mind, cruel and relentless, refusing him even a moment of peace. She had opened her heart, believing in him completely, while he had selfishly chased illusions.

He searched the room with restless eyes, avoiding the sleeping figure behind him. Spotting his shirt carelessly tossed onto the floor near the chair, Tony picked it up, feeling suddenly weary as he pulled it on. It felt colder now, heavier somehow—as if stitched together from disappointment rather than fabric.

***

Vasily stared blankly at the stack of unpaid bills scattered across his desk and rubbed his temples to ease his growing headache. He knew it was only a matter of time before his carefully maintained façade of wealth would collapse, leaving him exposed and humiliated. Lately, every knock on the door seemed to echo with a hidden threat.

Another hesitant knock distracted Vasily from his gloomy thoughts. He sighed deeply, adjusted his jacket to maintain a semblance of composure, and called irritably, "Come in."

The door swung open, and Tony stepped into the office. Vasily raised his eyebrows, momentarily startled by this unexpected visitor.

Tony nodded politely, a cautious but determined expression on his face. "Hello, Vasily. Mind if we talk?"

"Of course," Vasily replied, slowly rising and extending his hand. He quickly pushed aside some paperwork and gestured toward the chair across from his desk. "What's on your mind?"

"Look," Tony began, sitting down and leaning forward slightly, "I've been thinking a lot about your plans for the monastery restoration. I've decided I want in—I'm ready to invest."

Vasily's breath caught. These were words he'd hoped—no, prayed—to hear. A wave of relief washed over him, quickly followed by cautious skepticism. He couldn't afford to sound too eager.

"This is...unexpected," Vasily said slowly, choosing his words carefully. "I got the impression you weren't exactly thrilled with the idea when we spoke last."

Tony shrugged, a small smile appearing on his lips. "Things change, Vasily. People change. I've realized it's time for me to start fresh, and this project feels right."

This time, Vasily couldn't help but smile genuinely. Tony's offer was like a lifeline thrown just in time. "Well, Tony, I have to admit—you just saved my neck."

Tony chuckled softly. "We help each other out, man. I need a reliable partner in Kiev, and you need funds. Seems like fate, doesn't it?"

Vasily nodded thoughtfully. Fate. Perhaps it was indeed fate, though fate had a twisted sense of humor, pairing a Ukrainian who'd spent his life pretending to have money with an American who actually had it yet struggled with ambivalence.

As they talked, the secretary brought tea—strong, bitter, yet oddly comforting. Tony sipped it slowly, studying Vasily carefully as the Ukrainian described his ambitious vision for rebuilding the Kiev-Pechersk Monastery. Tony sensed a sincere desperation beneath Vasily's enthusiasm and felt a surprising empathy. Vasily's bravado mirrored his own inner turmoil.

Gradually, the tension between them eased, giving way to a more comfortable, almost friendly atmosphere. Tony found himself genuinely drawn to Vasily's passion, while Vasily felt a cautious spark of optimism for the first time in months.

Still, an invisible barrier remained. Their laughter occasionally faltered, their eyes drifted off into silence. Deep down, both men were acutely aware of their fundamental differences, intuitively sensing that this partnership—however promising—was built on shaky ground.

When Tony finally stood up to leave, Vasily grasped his hand warmly, sincerely. "Thank you, Tony. You have no idea how much I needed this."

"I think I do," Tony replied steadily, meeting Vasily's gaze. "This is a fresh start for both of us. Let's make it count."

After Tony left the room, Vasily stood quietly, feeling hope tempered by anxiety. Despite their newfound camaraderie, he couldn't shake the uneasy feeling that they still misunderstood each other, driven by motives they hadn't fully acknowledged or even realized.

Outside, Tony took a deep breath, letting the crisp air sharpen his senses. He silently reflected on his decisions. He'd reached out to Vasily partly out of desperation, partly because of Vera—but something deeper inside whispered that this choice might take him down a road he wasn't fully prepared for.

Yet, despite the unsettling premonition, Tony couldn't ignore the exhilaration building inside him. This felt like the start of something real, something meaningful.

He glanced up at Vasily's office window, noticing the man still watching him from above. Tony nodded silently before walking away.

Chapter 37

It was around four in the afternoon when Vera quietly entered her brother's office. Tony was in the conference room, absorbed in conversation with a team of architects, his hands gesturing animatedly over a pile of blueprints.

"Good afternoon, Vera," the secretary said warmly, standing up to greet her. "Should I let Vasily Petrovich know you're here?"

"No, thank you," Vera smiled gently, adjusting the strap of her purse. "I'll just wait."

She moved to the large window overlooking Kiev's busy streets. Her reflection stared back at her—tired eyes. She didn't even hear Tony approaching until she felt his hands gently rest upon her shoulders.

"I'm glad you're here," he whispered softly.

Vera turned around slowly, looking up at him with a quiet intensity. "Tomorrow, you'll be gone." Her voice faltered. "Doesn't feel real yet."

Tony met her eyes, struggling to hide the ache he felt inside. "There's one more thing I need to do before I leave. Want to join me?"

Vera nodded silently. Something in his voice unsettled her, yet she didn't dare ask what.

When they reached Kiev-Pechersk Monastery, the warm sun spilled golden light over the ancient domes, the bells chiming softly like distant music. Yet, beneath the surface, a strange anxiety buzzed in the air. Tony held Vera's hand tighter than usual as they descended into the Near Caves.

"You didn't even get to see all of Kiev," Vera said softly, almost apologetically. "You missed seeing the places in your grandfather's photographs."

Tony offered a comforting smile, masking the regret in his voice. "Next time, Vera. We'll see everything together."

"Next time," she echoed quietly, wondering bitterly if life ever granted second chances.

The narrow tunnels soon swallowed them in darkness, broken only by the faint flicker of candles lining the rough stone walls. The air grew heavy and damp, pressing against their skin with cold, ghostly fingers. Tony felt goosebumps rise on his arms, but he brushed it off, focusing instead on Vera's quiet presence beside him.

"How exactly did Saint Anthony die?" Tony asked, his voice breaking the oppressive silence.

"In his final years," Vera began slowly, carefully choosing her words, "Anthony rarely left these caves. Pilgrims would sometimes hear his voice, but few actually saw him. He spent his last days praying alone. Chronicles say he died on July twenty-third, one-thousand and seventy-three, during Prince Svyatoslav Yaroslavich's reign."

Tony whistled softly. "That's incredible. Think of all the history he witnessed—the rise and fall of dynasties."

Vera nodded thoughtfully. "He lived through an entire century. Some people here believe he died even later, at the age of a hundred and five."

Tony shook his head in amazement. "Sounds like Anthony lived not just one life, but several."

They had drifted deeper into the labyrinth of tunnels without noticing. Shadows stretched along the walls like distorted, watchful figures. Tony's breath quickened slightly, a faint unease gnawing at his gut.

"Only a select few were permitted to see Anthony in prayer or meditation," Vera continued quietly. "Even the monks who recorded his death never explicitly called him dead."

"What?" Tony halted suddenly. "Then how did they—"

"They believed Anthony stayed alive through his teachings. His voice, his wisdom—never really died. Some swore they saw him in Constantinople, hiring icon painters. Legend has it he paid in gold himself. Others claim he's buried in Rome by Saint Peter's grave. Nobody knows what's true anymore."

"But that doesn't make sense," Tony argued, voice edged with frustration. "If he died here, somebody had to have seen his body."

"That's the thing," Vera whispered, her voice trembling slightly. "Nobody did. When he stopped answering, they simply walled up his cave. No one dared disturb the saint's resting place."

A cold shiver crawled up Tony's spine. He grabbed Vera's hand tighter, feeling her pulse flutter anxiously against his fingertips.

They passed a faded wooden sign reading "Do Not Enter," its lettering chipped and nearly illegible. Suddenly, from the shadowed depths, an old monk emerged, hobbling toward them on an uneven gait. His face, etched with age and sternness, was distorted with anger.

"Who allowed you down here?" he barked sharply in heavily accented English, raising his frail hands as if to ward them off. "Tourists aren't permitted! Get out immediately!"

Tony stepped protectively in front of Vera, unsure how to react. The monk advanced, eyes blazing fiercely.

But then, from behind, a deep, authoritative voice echoed clearly through the passageway: "Let them pass."

At once, the old monk froze. He bowed reverently and moved aside.

Tony turned, squinting into the darkness, but saw only the vague silhouette of a figure shrouded in black. The stranger's hair and beard fell long around him, blending seamlessly into the surrounding gloom.

"Thank you," Vera murmured shakily, her voice barely audible, gripping Tony's hand as she pulled him forward.

As they continued, Tony glanced back nervously. The old monk stared after them, troubled and uncertain.

"What if they find something they're not meant to?" he muttered fearfully.

Again, the commanding voice resonated through the catacombs: "She prevented him from defiling this sacred place and dishonoring our ancestors. Let them go."

The monk bowed deeper, trembling visibly, his silhouette disappearing into the shadows.

Tony and Vera hurried forward, hearts pounding. The candlelight flickered ominously, creating dancing shadows on the cold stone walls.

"What just happened?" Tony whispered.

"I don't know," Vera replied softly, pressing closer to him, her breath shallow.

The tunnels around them seemed endless, ancient, and alive. The silence stretched heavily between them, each step resonating like a heartbeat echoing into eternity.

Finally, they reached a narrow stairway ascending toward faint sunlight. Vera paused, glancing back one last time into the catacombs' profound darkness.

"Some secrets," she whispered, "should remain buried."

***

The rays of the setting sun sliced through the heavy clouds, spilling liquid gold over the domes of the Kiev-Pechersk Monastery. For a moment, Tony stood motionless, captivated by the quiet grandeur before him. He could feel the history beneath his feet and hear the whispers of monks who had walked these same grounds centuries before.

Slowly kneeling down, Tony touched the earth gently, almost reverently. The soil felt cool and strangely alive between his fingers. He took a careful handful and placed it gently into a small plastic bag.

Only now, as he held that modest bit of Ukrainian earth in his hands, did he begin to grasp the true meaning behind his grandfather's mysterious will. It wasn't about money or hidden treasure. It was about roots and memory, about the bond that ties generations together despite distance, time, or misunderstanding.

Tony stood up, his throat tight with an emotion he could hardly define. His gaze wandered toward the monastery walls, the graceful silhouettes of trees, and the city spreading out gently beneath the hills. A strange calmness enveloped him. In this moment, he felt as though he'd finally come home—not to a place of wealth or material comfort, but to something deeper, more enduring, and infinitely more valuable.

He glanced at the bag of soil in his hand, feeling its symbolic weight. This handful of earth was not just dirt. It was a memory. It was identity. It was an inheritance far richer than gold.

Above him, the monastery bells began to softly toll, their clear, solemn tones rippling through the evening air. Tony closed his eyes briefly, letting the sound wash over him like a blessing, a farewell, or perhaps—a new beginning.

Chapter 38

Despite the warm sunlight streaming through the expansive windows, Tony felt a chill from the sterile brightness of the departure lounge. Around them, travelers bustled, each absorbed in their own journeys.

Vasily glanced impatiently at the flight announcement board, breaking the uneasy silence. Vera stood quietly next to Tony, gripping her purse tightly.

"They just announced boarding for your flight," Vera finally whispered, barely audible over the noise of the airport.

Tony forced a smile and turned to Vasily, feigning confidence. "Well, at least I know who to hit up back in the States. I may not have all the cash myself, but trust me—I'll round up investors. Your project's got legs."

Vasily chuckled, waving him off with exaggerated ease though his eyes betrayed hidden worry. "Don't sweat it, man. If the investment works out, it's fantastic. If it doesn't—well, money has a funny way of showing up when you need it most. Besides," he added, shooting a meaningful glance at Vera, "what matters is that you come back. I've gotten used to having you around—you're damn good company. And someone here is gonna miss you something fierce."

Vera blushed softly, her gaze glued to Tony as if trying to etch his face into memory.

"I'll, uh—give you two a minute," Vasily said knowingly, tipping an imaginary hat. "Coffee's calling my name anyway."

As Vasily disappeared into the crowd, Vera turned to Tony, eyes shining with barely restrained tears. Tony reached out, gently brushing a loose strand of hair from her face.

"You know, Vera," Tony murmured softly, emotion cracking his voice, "you're the best thing that ever happened to me. You taught me how to love. I honestly don't know how I'm supposed to go back to life without you."

She looked into his eyes, wanting desperately to memorize this moment. He cupped her face gently, kissing her softly, oblivious to everything else in the bustling terminal. Finally, Vera pulled back, dabbing at her eyes and quickly reaching into her purse.

"I want you to have something," she said, carefully handing Tony a photograph. "To make sure you don't forget me."

Tony took the picture, smiling sadly at her radiant image. "Believe me, Vera, I won't need a photograph to remember you."

Vasily returned, sipping his coffee and giving them a knowing look. "Hey, lover boy, hate to rush the goodbyes, but your flight won't wait forever."

Tony reluctantly grabbed his carry-on, casting one last look at Vera.

As he approached security, he placed his bag on the conveyor belt. A broad-shouldered guard scrutinized his belongings, moving slowly, methodically. Tony glanced impatiently at his watch, feeling a ripple of anxiety as the line grew behind him.

The guard suddenly paused, holding up the small plastic bag filled with dark earth. His eyes narrowed suspiciously. "What's this?" he demanded sharply, shaking the bag.

"It's just soil," Tony said, forcing a casual tone, though his stomach twisted. "You know—a keepsake from Ukraine."

The guard scowled deeply, clearly irritated. "You trying to play games with me? Who carries dirt as a souvenir? Passport—now. You're coming with me."

Tony's pulse quickened. "Hey, come on, it's sentimental...there's nothing—"

"I said, now," the guard interrupted curtly, voice raised enough that heads turned toward them.

From the waiting area, Vera anxiously grabbed her brother's sleeve. "Something's wrong," she whispered, her voice trembling.

Vasily frowned deeply, moving forward as if ready to intervene. "Maybe I should talk to someone—"

But before they could react, security personnel swiftly ushered Tony into a side room. The door closed firmly behind him, leaving him alone, heart pounding, trapped with his thoughts and the sharp realization of how quickly dreams could unravel.

***

Tony stood awkwardly in his boxers inside the cramped inspection room, shifting from foot to foot, watching helplessly as the Ukrainian security officers tore through his bags. The senior officer thumbed slowly through Tony's passport, glancing suspiciously at him every few seconds.

Tony glanced down at his Rolex anxiously. "Hey guys, can we speed this up? I've got a flight boarding right now."

The irritated guard ignored him completely and tossed the small plastic bag of soil onto the metal table. Soil spilled across the table and floor. "Get dressed," he finally barked.

Tony hastily pulled his pants on, jamming items haphazardly back into his carry-on. He sprinted toward the departure gates, his bag still half-unzipped.

"Final boarding call for Lufthansa flight to Frankfurt," the PA system announced loudly.

"Oh, perfect," Tony muttered sarcastically, picking up speed.

He reached passport control breathlessly and handed his documents to the bored official behind the desk, who regarded him suspiciously over rimmed glasses.

"What was the purpose of your visit to Ukraine?" the officer asked, taking his sweet time.

Tony forced a strained smile, tapping his fingers impatiently on the counter. "Just tourism. Look, my plane—"

"Relax," the man said flatly as he leisurely stamped Tony's passport. He returned it with an indifferent shrug.

"Thanks a bunch," Tony snapped, grabbing the documents.

At security screening, the metal detector went off loudly. Tony groaned audibly.

"Step back, please," the guard said calmly.

"Are you kidding me right now?" Tony grumbled, removing his belt, shoes, and gold watch hastily, nearly dropping them. The guard merely shrugged, unbothered. "Sorry, sir. It's for your safety."

Tony finally cleared security, muttering loudly, "Safety, my ass. I'm so done with this country."

As he dashed toward the gate, his half-open bag flapping wildly, a familiar high-pitched voice stopped him cold.

"Tony! Tony, is that you?"

Before he could even turn fully, Zhenya wrapped her arms around his neck, enveloping him in a cloud of perfume. Svetka stood nearby, grinning mischievously.

"We thought they'd thrown you in jail or something!" Zhenya giggled, planting a sticky kiss on his neck.

"Or that you'd found yourself another Ukrainian girl," Svetka teased, playfully adjusting his rumpled shirt collar.

Tony felt his face grow hot. "Oh, wow, ladies! Great to see you again, really— but I'm gonna miss my plane."

Zhenya pouted theatrically, finally letting go of his arm. "Don't forget us, Tony!"

Tony quickly kissed her on the nose and Svetka on the cheek. "How could I ever forget?"

Ignoring the curious looks from passing passengers, he sprinted the last few meters toward the gate just as the attendant was about to close the door.

"I'm here, I'm here!" he gasped, nearly tripping over his own feet.

The attendant raised an eyebrow, smiled slightly, and let him through. Tony stumbled down the aisle, dropping heavily into his seat. His hair was disheveled, his shirt untucked, and faint lipstick marks adorned his cheek.

Tony let out a deep breath, shaking his head with a weary smile. "Jesus," he muttered to himself, straightening his tie. "What a country."

The man beside him yawned indifferently, clearly uninterested in Tony's misadventures. Tony leaned over slightly and added, "More stuff happens in one day here than an entire lifetime back home."

Chapter 39

Vasily exhaled with visible relief, loosening his tie as they walked away from the bustling terminal. The noise of Borispol Airport quickly faded behind them, leaving only a tense silence.

"Thank God he's gone," Vasily murmured, glancing briefly at Vera.

"Gone..." she whispered, her voice barely audible. Her eyes were fixed on the distant dot of Tony's plane, which gradually dissolved into the sky.

Vasily fidgeted uneasily with his keys as they approached the car.

"Vera, there's something I've always wanted to ask but never dared," he began, hesitating. He glanced at her nervously. "What exactly is hidden in Anthony's grave?"

"Nothing," Vera replied simply, staring straight ahead.

"Nothing?" Vasily echoed incredulously, opening the car door for her. "You're telling me that a thousand years of legends, intrigue, and whispers in the shadows… and it was empty all along? Just dust?"

Vera settled quietly into the passenger seat, her gaze distant. "No one will ever find Saint Anthony's relics. Never."

"Why?" Vasily asked, turning the ignition. His knuckles whitened as he gripped the steering wheel tightly.

"Because Anthony himself decreed it," she answered calmly, her voice low and certain. "His final wish was that no eyes should ever look upon his remains."

Vasily shook his head in frustration as the car merged onto the highway. Dark clouds were gathering above Kiev, and sunlight struck through in sharp, dramatic rays, illuminating the city in patches of gold and shadow.

"So all this secrecy is just to hide the truth?" he asked sharply. "To protect some image?"

"No, not just an image—an entire faith," Vera said, her voice heavy with significance. "The true test of sainthood always comes after death, not during life."

"What do you mean?" Vasily demanded, clearly uncomfortable.

Vera turned slowly toward her brother. "One year after death, the saint's bones are exhumed. If they're perfectly clean, the person's sainthood is proven. If not, it reveals hidden sins. Anthony knew this, Vasily. Imagine if the founder of Russian monasticism failed such a test."

Vasily stared blankly ahead, gripping the steering wheel harder. "It would've destroyed people's faith."

"Exactly," Vera whispered, gazing thoughtfully out the window. "Anthony feared that his entire life's work could collapse in an instant if even a single flaw was revealed. He couldn't risk it. And so, no one was ever allowed to see."

Vasily was silent for a moment, the lines of his face taut. Finally, he spoke, bitterness edging into his voice. "No one saw Christ's body either. Convenient, isn't it? I always wondered what really happened there. Perhaps they feared exactly the same test."

Vera's eyes flashed, emotion breaking through her calm exterior. "Two thousand years ago or now—does it matter? People always seek truth, but truth can be dangerous, Vasily. Faith is fragile."

They fell into silence, the car speeding toward Kiev. Ahead, the Kiev-Pechersk Monastery loomed, its golden domes luminous against the gathering storm clouds. They appeared both beautiful and tragic, like silent sentinels of history's secrets.

"Tell me," Vasily said abruptly, turning toward her. "Who was supposed to open Anthony's grave?"

"Feodosiy, Anthony's closest disciple," Vera replied quietly.

Vasily hesitated, glancing at her sharply. "But Feodosiy died before Anthony, didn't he? That's convenient, too."

"Yes, he died two months before Antony. Perhaps fate—or perhaps someone intervened to protect Antony's secret."

"Then how did you figure all this out?" Vasily asked quietly, slowing the car slightly as they neared the Dnieper Bridge.

Vera's expression turned distant, mysterious. "I had help."

He suddenly swerved to the roadside, pulling the car to an abrupt stop. Turning fully toward her, Vasily's voice shook with suppressed anxiety. "Tell me honestly, Vera—what awaits Ukraine?"

Vera met her brother's gaze directly, unflinching. Her voice carried the quiet certainty of a prophecy. "Either Ukraine returns fully to the faith and spirit of its ancestors, or it will vanish entirely. There is no third option."

Vasily felt his breath catch in his throat. "How can you say something like that so calmly?"

"Because it's the truth," Vera replied softly, her eyes filled with sorrowful determination. "The past warns us clearly, Vasily. Anthony's secret, Christ's hidden body—these mysteries teach us that faith is tested most fiercely when truth and belief collide. Ukraine stands at such a crossroads now."

Outside, thunder rumbled softly in the distance, and the first raindrops splashed against the windshield.

Vasily started the engine again, gripping the wheel tightly as they drove onward. He glanced toward the monastery's golden domes once more, illuminated like beacons amidst the storm.

"Do you really believe Ukraine will survive?" he asked quietly, almost fearfully.

Vera placed a gentle hand on his arm, her voice steady and full of hope despite the darkness surrounding them.

"I believe Ukraine will endure—but not without pain."

Chapter 40

Chicago. Tony was finally home.

When he stepped inside, his apartment felt oddly frozen in time—as if no one had lived there for years, despite only being gone two weeks. The silence was oppressive. A thin layer of dust had settled on the surfaces. Beer sat untouched in the fridge, pillows lay scattered across his bed just as he'd left them, and everything else waited exactly where it always had.

Standing in the doorway, Tony felt like a traveler stepping back into a past life. The memories of Ukraine were still vivid, and yet already they seemed distant, almost unreal.

As he unpacked slowly in his living room, Tony caught sight of the city outside his window. Chicago's familiar skyline, cold and indifferent, stared back at him. On his taxi ride home from O'Hare, he'd found himself searching for echoes of Kiev in these familiar streets: a glimpse of an ancient cathedral, the ringing of distant church bells, or simply the warmth he'd felt standing beside Vera. But he saw only polished steel and glass towers, bustling traffic, and faces rushing to destinations unknown.

Cross-legged on the carpet, Tony sifted through his luggage, unpacking mechanically. Suddenly, a small plastic bag slipped from his grasp onto the floor, nearly empty. His pulse quickened slightly as he picked it up, carefully pouring the remaining grains of soil into the palm of his hand.

He stared silently at the earth—so simple, and yet carrying the weight of generations, history, and faith. Tony tightened his grip, holding the last tangible remnant of his journey, his grandfather's dying wish now resting in his palm.

Closing his eyes, he felt a deep ache in his chest. Somewhere far across the ocean, the ancient city he'd left behind was going on without him.

***

It was late in the evening when Tony entered Graceland Cemetery. He walked slowly, guided only by the faint glow of distant streetlamps filtering through the trees.

Reaching his grandfather's grave, Tony knelt down carefully, feeling the damp earth beneath him. He opened his palm slowly, reverently, watching as the dark Ukrainian soil gently spilled onto the cold Chicago ground. The granules blended seamlessly into the grave, bridging continents, lifetimes, and memories.

"It's done," Tony whispered, more to himself than anyone else. "I brought you back home, Grandpa."

He felt a powerful sense of release, as though a burden he'd been carrying for years had finally lifted. The circle had closed, the journey his grandfather wished him to take now complete. Tony finally understood the hidden message of the will—it wasn't about money or treasure but roots and belonging.

Just then, a sudden gust of wind rushed through the cemetery. Tony stood motionless, eyes closed, breathing in deeply. The cold air stung his face, but he hardly noticed. For the first time in his life, he felt truly connected—both to his past and to something far greater than himself.

***

On the other side of the world, Vera walked slowly along the ancient walls of the Kiev-Pechersk Monastery. The sun had already dipped below the horizon, leaving only a pale purple glow lingering in the twilight sky. The monastery's gold-domed churches stood solemn and silent, their silhouettes sharply etched against the fading light.

A sudden gust of wind swept through the courtyard, gently lifting Vera's hair and sending an unexpected chill through her body. She stopped, breathing deeply to steady herself, her eyes drifting across the centuries-old stones as if seeking answers from their silent strength.

Never had she felt such loneliness—not simply an absence, but a deep, persistent ache settling within her heart. It was a sadness she could neither escape nor soothe, as though some essential part of herself had vanished along with Tony, leaving only shadows and silence behind.

Chapter 41

"Congratulations!" Grandpa's lawyer said warmly, shaking Tony's hand with his familiar professional smile. "Now you can access the money anytime, and do whatever you like with it."

Tony stood silently in the lawyer's office, noticing that it didn't seem as dull and gray as before. Even the lawyer himself no longer appeared quite as dry and boring as Tony had remembered.

"Thank you," Tony replied thoughtfully. He raised his head and looked directly into the lawyer's eyes. "But I still don't get it. Can I ask you something?"

The lawyer raised his eyebrows, listening intently.

"How exactly did Grandpa get this money? I mean, he wasn't wealthy, not by any stretch of the imagination. His job never paid much, and after he retired he barely left the house. How could he have possibly saved up so much in such a short time?"

The lawyer smiled gently. "Your grandfather made his fortune investing in the stock market. It became his hobby after retirement. He began trading stocks from virtually nothing, and—remarkably—achieved extraordinary returns. His intuition was truly uncanny; somehow he always knew exactly where to put his money. Honestly, I'm probably the only person who wasn't surprised when he decided to pass his fortune to you."

Tony nodded slowly. A sudden wave of embarrassment washed over him. It hurt to realize just how little he truly knew or understood his grandfather.

After a pause, Tony spoke up again. "Could I ask you to manage my finances the same way you managed Grandpa's?"

The lawyer's face softened visibly, breaking into a genuine, warm smile—the first authentic smile Tony had ever seen from him. Without his usual professional mask, he appeared completely different: relaxed, confident, but with a faint sadness lingering in his eyes.

Tony hesitated before continuing, carefully choosing his words. "Listen, this may sound personal, and I apologize in advance, but... what exactly is your background?"

The lawyer took a deep breath, seeming unsurprised, as if he'd long anticipated this question. "Well, I'm an American—officially, anyway. But my roots are French. I spend a week or two in Paris every year. France was my family's home, although most of my relatives were killed by the Nazis during World War II, fighting to protect their homeland."

He gazed thoughtfully out the window, lost momentarily in memories. "After the war, about two-thirds of Western European immigrants who'd fled to America returned home. I stayed here, though. Life just unfolded that way. America became my home, and now my children and grandchildren live here. Maybe they're luckier than we are. They don't know the ache of homesickness—the quiet pain of always feeling divided between two worlds."

He turned slowly back to Tony, eyes filled with compassion. "Your grandfather understood something important, something most people don't realize. By fulfilling his final wish, you inherited something far more valuable than money."

Tony stared, suddenly comprehending. "A handful of soil..."

"Exactly," the lawyer said softly, smiling gently. "You inherited a connection to your ancestors, their homeland, their beliefs, perhaps even their capacity for love. In all my years, I've never executed a more generous will."

Tony was stunned. He suddenly realized the magnitude of the mistake he'd nearly made. "You knew exactly what Grandpa meant from the very start? And yet you let me run around

Ukraine looking for gold and treasure, nearly desecrating a saint's grave? Why didn't you warn me?"

The lawyer gave a rueful half-smile, his voice calm yet firm. "Because some things can't be explained with words. Any man can bend down and pick up a handful of soil—but not every man can hear the voice of his ancestors speaking through it."

Chapter 42

Tony wandered slowly along the shore of Lake Michigan, the cold breeze from the lake biting into his skin. He watched the seagulls wheel above him, their cries blending with the rhythmic slap of waves against the rocks. A sharp ache twisted inside his chest—he couldn't get Vera out of his mind. Almost a month without her, and every day dragged on like an eternity. It was as if he'd left part of himself behind in Kiev.

For a second, his thoughts strayed to Sofia. But that had just been a fling—a temporary distraction—and they'd both known it. With Vera, it was different.

He couldn't take it anymore. In a rush, Tony grabbed his phone, his fingers shaking slightly as he dialed Vera's number. The ringing felt endless until he finally heard her voice, quiet and cautious.

"Tony?"

"Vera, thank God—I need you to listen to me." He took a deep breath, his voice raw with desperation. "I can't do this anymore. I thought I'd get back to Chicago, fall into my routine, and things would make sense again, but they don't. Nothing makes sense without you."

There was a pause, heavy with silence, and Tony felt his pulse racing.

"Tony—" she started gently.

"Please, Vera," he interrupted. "You're like the air I breathe. You never realize how badly you need it until it's gone. And right now, I'm suffocating. Please, come to Chicago. I'll show you everything—you'll fall head over heels for this city. It's got beauty, it's got life—but none of it means a damn thing without you here."

Vera sighed softly, her voice tight with emotion. "Tony, you know I can't. America is your home. You were born there, you built your life there. My place is here, in Ukraine. You can't just uproot yourself and expect me to do the same. We all have our own paths, and this—this isn't mine."

Tony shook his head as though she could see him, frustration gnawing at his heart. "Vera, stop. Listen, I already sent the paperwork—the invitation—to the American Embassy in Kiev. It's all arranged; you just need to go pick it up, get your visa. It'll take an hour, tops, and then you'll be on your way to me. Can't we just give this a shot?"

"Tony, you're not hearing me—"

"No, Vera, you're not hearing me," he pleaded, almost desperate now. "Every damn moment I'm awake, all I think about is you and Ukraine. You turned my world upside down, and now I can't just flip a switch and go back to the way things were. Please, Vera—give us a chance."

The wind picked up suddenly, drowning out Vera's soft breathing on the other end of the line. Tony waited, heart hammering, praying she might finally give in. But when she spoke again, her voice was barely a whisper, filled with tenderness and sadness.

"Tony, if you truly love me, you'll understand that asking me to leave is asking me to lose myself. I wish it could be different, but it isn't. I'm so sorry..."

Her voice trailed away. Tony stared at the restless waves as the realization hit him like a freight train: he'd finally found the woman he couldn't live without, only to realize that their worlds were oceans apart.

Chapter 43

Tony sat across from Michael in his friend's plush corner office, high above Chicago's bustling Loop. Beyond the panoramic windows, skyscrapers stood like gray sentinels beneath a steel-colored sky, their glass facades mirroring the gloomy clouds above. Michael leaned back in his leather chair, hands clasped behind his head, perfectly at ease. Tony envied that certainty.

"Tony, are you out of your mind? Ukraine is in financial quicksand. You put cash into that country, and it's gone—poof—just like that. High crime, endless corruption... You'd be better off lighting your dollars on fire and roasting marshmallows."

Tony shook his head sharply, frustration flashing across his face.

"Come on, Mike. You've thrown money at places just as shady. Half of South America, for God's sake. Why suddenly draw the line at Ukraine?"

Michael's eyes narrowed as he leaned in further, his voice firm.

"I never play with loaded dice, Tony. My investors trust me because I don't gamble with their cash. Money doesn't have feelings—it wants stability, period. It doesn't give a damn if the country's fascist, communist, or capitalist. Money respects one thing and one thing only: stability. And Ukraine? It's as stable as a drunk on a tightrope."

Tony stood abruptly, pacing to the large world map on the wall. He stared at it for a moment, tracing a finger slowly along the outline of Eastern Europe. After a long pause, he turned, catching Michael's puzzled gaze.

"Mike, remind me again—where are your people from?"

Michael blinked, taken aback by the shift in the conversation. "Come again? What's that got to do with anything?"

"I'm asking about your family roots. Indulge me for a second."

Michael's expression softened slightly as he sighed.

"You know perfectly well, Tony. My great-grandfather came from Italy and landed at Ellis Island with fifty bucks in his pocket. Italian-American all the way."

Tony held his friend's gaze steadily. "And tell me, Mike—do you invest in Italy?"

Michael paused, slightly uncomfortable. He tugged at his silk tie. "Yeah, but that's completely different. I've got connections there, family who'd have my back in a heartbeat."

Tony gave him a knowing smile, his eyebrows raised pointedly.

"And you think I don't have connections in Ukraine? Mike, I'm not asking you to risk your investors' money—I'm talking about my own cash. My skin in the game, my choice."

Michael exhaled loudly, shaking his head in exasperation. "Tony, you're skating on thin ice. I'm just trying to talk some sense into you before you plunge headfirst into disaster."

Tony was quiet for a moment, eyes drifting to a small model airplane perched on Michael's bookshelf. His voice became softer, edged with something deeper than mere business.

"Ever think about who we bomb, Mike?"

Michael sat up straight, caught off guard. "Who 'we'? What's that supposed to mean?"

"Us, Mike. America." Tony's voice hardened with intensity. "We bombed Yugoslavia. That's right, in Europe—places our ancestors could've walked through. Afghanistan, Iraq, Libya… Hell, half the world. Have you ever stopped to think our bombs might've fallen on places holding graves of distant relatives, innocent people related to Americans like us? Doesn't that ever eat at you?"

Michael waved dismissively.

"Come on, Tony, that's politics, not finance. It's above our pay grade."

Tony's voice rose.

"No, Mike, it's exactly our business. Our money buys those bombs. Our investments shape policy. Have you ever wondered why half the world hates our guts? Because you can't bomb the hell out of innocent people and expect gratitude in return. Freedom and democracy—those are words we slap on the cover story. Yugoslavia was about power, and Iraq was about oil. You don't need that Harvard MBA"—Tony jabbed a thumb at Michael's diplomas hanging proudly on the wall—"to see through that bullshit."

Michael threw up his hands, irritation flaring. "Jesus, Tony. I'm not the Pentagon or the White House. What do you want from me, anyway?"

A heavy silence fell between them. Tony stared at his friend. Finally, he spoke again, his voice quieter now, raw and honest.

"I just want you to open your damn eyes, Mike. This isn't just about numbers—it's about who we are, who we become."

He turned toward the door, gripping the handle. He paused again, the bitterness in his voice clear.

"You know, back in Kiev, I walked those streets. I met people who've tasted corruption, betrayal, and fear their whole lives.

But I also met people who have something we've lost: hope, heart, a sense of belonging that money can't buy."

Tony turned the knob.

"Money might buy stability, Mike, but it can't buy your soul back."

The door clicked shut softly behind him.

Chapter 44

Tony sat quietly beside his mother's favorite flowers, sheltered under the wide branches of the old spruce tree in the backyard. The warm, familiar scent of lilacs and freshly cut grass filled the air, carrying him back to his childhood. Everything here breathed a calm and gentle peace—or perhaps it simply felt this way because his mother was beside him.

"Mom," Tony finally spoke, breaking the silence, "I've transferred half the money into your account. The rest... Well, I decided to invest it in Ukraine."

"You've decided to go back," she replied softly, her voice weary yet strangely calm. "Your grandfather always said graves were like magnets—they pull you closer no matter how far you stray. I'm just beginning to understand what he meant."

Tony noticed the slight tremble in her shoulders. It wasn't from cold, he knew, but from the quiet ache of worry that only mothers truly understood. He hesitated, wanting desperately to ease her mind.

"Mom, please come with me," he said gently, covering her fragile hand with his own. "We can go together. Ukraine—it changed something inside me. It might change you, too."

A faint smile appeared on her lips, tinged with sadness. She shook her head slightly, eyes gazing into the distance. "No, Tony. It's too late for me. You can't uproot old trees, and besides..." Her voice faded to a whisper, "the graves of everyone I loved are right here. Someone needs to look after them. The dead—they never feel gone. They're always somewhere nearby, waiting quietly for someone to come and say hello."

Tony's heart clenched. He felt helpless before the gentle certainty of his mother's words.

After a brief silence, she continued, gazing thoughtfully at the flowers. "A person can live their entire life without ever wondering about their past. But one day, at some crossroads, something pushes them out of a warm, comfortable bed, and suddenly they're traveling to places they never thought they'd see. At first, it seems random, just a strange urge. But soon, they realize something powerful. Certain places feel inexplicably warm—like crawling back into your childhood bed after a long, exhausting journey. Those places might even be dangerous for the body, but they comfort the soul like nothing else can."

She turned toward Tony, her eyes gentle yet piercing. "Logic can't explain everything, son. But anyone who's felt the voice of their ancestors calling from a handful of soil understands exactly what I mean."

Tony shook his head, confusion clouding his face. "But Mom—what am I supposed to do there? I'm just...an ordinary guy." His voice dropped to a whisper, and he bent down to scoop up a handful of the soft, damp soil beneath their feet. "What could possibly come from a handful of soil?"

His mother reached out slowly, gently stroking his hair—just like she did when he was a small boy, afraid of the dark. She hadn't touched him like that in years, and the gesture brought tears to Tony's eyes. Her voice was soft, yet strong enough.

"The entire planet, Tony, is made from a handful of soil. Even the tallest mountain starts as dust. Your grandfather always said: 'Trust your heart, your mind, your soul—and never fear what they ask of you. ' Remember Moses from the Bible? He had everything—wealth, comfort, security. Yet he stepped out into uncertainty, risking everything because he heard a call deep inside him. He had a purpose greater than himself. And maybe..." Her voice faltered. "Maybe you have your own purpose, too."

Tony lowered his head, his fingers still clutching the cool earth, as he let her words settle inside him.

She gently cupped his face in her hands, looking deeply into his eyes. "You're young, Tony. Your entire life lies ahead of you. Follow what moves your soul. Don't be afraid of the road it takes you down—even if it's uncertain, even if it seems impossible."

Epilogue

Michael's car turned onto Tony's street. He couldn't shake the uneasy feeling that had stayed with him ever since their last conversation. Tony hadn't called or dropped by the office since then, and Sofia hadn't heard from him either. The unusual silence was starting to get under Michael's skin.

The car stopped in front of Tony's familiar apartment building, and Sofia got out of the car, exchanging puzzled glances as they scanned the list of names by the front door. Tony's name wasn't there.

Just then, a woman in her forties stepped out of the building.

"Excuse me," Michael called out with a friendly wave. "Have you seen Tony around lately?"

The neighbor paused and gave him an odd look. "You don't know? Tony put his apartment up for sale and moved to Ukraine."

Michael stared at Sofia, dumbfounded. Tony wouldn't have just left without a goodbye... would he?

When the woman walked away, Sofia finally broke the tense silence. "Michael, what do you think this means?"

Michael stayed quiet.

Sofia pressed further. "Tony has always been selfish. He's never cared about anyone but himself."

Michael shook his head dismissively. "Don't let it get to you. Tony's just under some romantic illusion about Ukraine right now. Trust me, the spell will wear off quickly. He'll realize there's nothing to do in Ukraine—it's a dead place. Besides, with such a level of corruption, this country will quickly fall apart and become mired in civil war."

Sofia turned away sharply, frustration in her eyes. Michael glanced upward, watching the airplanes streak across the sky above the city. He wondered bitterly if one of them carried Tony far away—chasing dreams he could never understand.

***

Tony sat in the airplane cabin, poring over his grandfather's photos and documents, deep in thought. Suddenly, his heart raced when he came across Vera's portrait, the same one she had given him on the painful day he had left Kiev. The mere sight of her took his breath away. Tony smiled softly, remembering the warmth of her touch, the tenderness of her kiss.

He turned back to the picture of his grandfather, studying his aged face with quiet awe.

What was Tony thinking about at that moment? Maybe he thought about the fate of his grandfather, about all of those who, like Grandpa, would never be able to return home because their homeland had turned its back on them. Yet they never turned away from Ukraine while they wandered around the world. They always remembered the country of their birth from their first to their last breath. Dying unknown in a foreign land under an unfamiliar sky, they spoke their last words in their native language.

ABOUT THE AUTHOR

Dr. Andrew V. Kudin is a Ukrainian-born American writer, essayist, and scholar, widely recognized for his insightful explorations into history, law, and the complexities of the human condition. Holding doctoral degrees in Philosophy and Religious Studies (1995) and Law (2020), Dr. Kudin has dedicated his life to uncovering historical truths, analyzing moral dilemmas, and advocating for justice.

Dr. Kudin is the author of numerous articles and novels, including How to Survive in Prison, A Game of Blind, The Black Suit, and Verdict, which have earned him wide recognition. His works, deeply grounded in historical scholarship and psychological analysis, illuminate the intricate nature of human relationships, power dynamics, and faith.

In recognition of his contributions to historical research and literature, as well as his active involvement in ethical and spiritual discourse, Dr. Kudin was honored by the Ukrainian Orthodox Church with the prestigious Order of Saint Prince Vladimir, 3rd degree. This award underscores the profound impact of his work in preserving historical memory and exploring society's moral foundations.

Through his writing, Dr. Kudin continues to challenge conventional narratives, illuminating the past with clarity and depth, and inspiring readers to seek truth and justice in an ever-changing world.